TRIAL
BY FIRE

Trial by Fire

Cover Design by The Book Brander
TheBookBrander.com
Content Edits: Sue Brown-Moore
SueBrownMoore.com
Copy Edits: Laurel C. Kriegler
laurelckriegler.wordpress.com
Print Formatting by Nina Pierce of Seaside Publications
NinaPierce.com/book-formatting/

First Edition
ISBN: 979-8-9867802-2-1

TRIAL BY FIRE

SILVERSTAR MATES

INTERGALACTIC DATING AGENCY

USA TODAY BESTSELLING AUTHOR

LEA KIRK

SFR by LEA KIRK

The Prophecy Series
(in chronological order)

Prophecy
Book One

Blue Christmas
A Prophecy Series Holiday Novella

Space Ranger
A Prophecy Series Short Story
(*newsletter exclusive*)

All of Me
A Prophecy Series Short Story

Salvation
Book Two

Collision
Book Three

Skylar's Gift
A Prophecy Series Novella

Paradox
(Coming Soon)

Silverstar Mates Series
(in recommended reading order)

Fly With Me
Above the Storm
Wing and a Prayer
Trial by Fire

PNR by LEA KIRK

Made for Her
Part of S. E. Smith's, The Worlds of Magic, New Mexico

ONE

———✴———

Elder Kai Firewing tread light-footed along the path to the meditation garden, alert for the presence of others in his clan. The sun-warmed Bezchian desert sand pushed between his toes with each step, a familiar comfort that did not soothe his anxiety today. He should not be here in this oasis at the center of his colony. The meditation garden was for deserving elders, and he was not deserving. Had not been so for the last fifty-five sun migrations.

A puff of a breeze flitted over his bare chest, rustling the lightweight fabric of his billowing yellow leggings. He flattened his lips into a straight line. How had everything gone so wrong so suddenly? For more than three lifetimes, he had excelled at matching mates for the four mortal clans of his home-world. Had joined families that would thrive together, be stronger in their collective attributes. Fulfilled his role in the ancient Bezchian tradition upheld by the elders of the Firewing clan: the long-lived phoenixes.

One day he had been fine. The next, every couple he had attempted to join lacked…something. An element, a spark, a flame of the heart…something utterly unnecessary to a successful mating. Yet its absence had crippled his ability to unify any couples, over and over, until Most Esteemed Elder Uri had stopped giving him assignments. That decision still stung worse than a fire wasp. But Uri was the eldest of the elders, and had the final word in such decisions.

Still, the memory of that missing element left a bitter taste in Kai's soul.

Seventy-three sun migrations into your third incarnation, and you are as useless as a sand roach.

He had been *born* to match mates. His failure to do so—multiple times—was tantamount to a scandal. He ground his teeth together. The elders of the Firewing clan had a reputation to uphold, by the air currents. How did such a *malady*—because there was no better word to describe it—happen to an otherwise young, healthy phoenix?

"Greetings, Elder Kai." The soft, murmured words snapped Kai from his thoughts.

A fledgling-sized elder approached from around the fountain at the garden's center, her golden-eyed gaze on the ground instead of meeting his.

He pulled his wings in close to his back, the tips of his primary feathers brushing the backs of his leggings, and gave her a respectful nod. "Greetings, Elder Ena."

Even though she presented as no more than ten sun migrations, she was older than him by three hundred, thanks to the miracle of rebirth every one hundred sun migrations. Some in the Firewing clan had lived as long as two thousand sun migrations. It was understandable why off-worlders were often confused by this, and hence the reason his kind preferred the solitude of the Bezchian deserts.

"May your meditations be insightful." Ena quickened her pace as she passed him, her red and orange leggings molding to her spindly legs with her burst of speed. No doubt eager to avoid conversation with one as fallen as he.

"Aye, and your matches always strong." As his once were.

Ena continued along the path, and Kai turned his attention to finding an available white stone meditation perch to sit on. There, the one snuggled between two ember-berry bushes seemed to be waiting for him. And it would be in the full sun for a while. His current form was not of an age to regenerate yet, but was old enough to appreciate the heat provided by Bezchi's star.

He settled on the warm stone, pulled up one leg at a time to sit cross-legged—not an easy feat for his aging body—and sighed out loud in bliss. The stone's heat penetrated the wispy fabric of his leggings and eased into his muscles. He rested his hands on his knees and closed his eyes. The familiar sensation of calm settled over him as he slipped into a trance.

The trick now was to connect with his own elusive inner peace through his nearly four lifetimes of memories. Easier to anticipate then to achieve, as usual…but wait. There was something…wavering mirages of green. *That* was different. There was not much that was green in the desert.

The mirages solidified into…bushes? Yes, they were bushes dotted with some sort of deep red, layered flowers unlike any he had ever seen before. He lowered his gaze to the ground under his feet. Also green and lush in a way that his home was not.

A large, stone-lined pond materialized several paces ahead, at the farthest end of which was a fountain of water spraying upward before falling back down in misty droplets. He should be able to hear its soft pattering, but only complete silence pressed against his ears. It was odd, and somewhat disconcerting.

What is this place?

An answer to that question seemed unlikely without so much as a hint of enlightenment or familiarity from this vision.

A patch of air between him and the pond shimmered and morphed into a figure, similar to a small Bezchian female, but without wings. How odd. He studied her from behind. The garment covering her form was most unusual. A lacey, cream colored, body-hugging sheath of some sort. It clung to her curves, flaring over her shapely backend and full hips, before ending mid-calf.

Why was he sharing this space with one clearly not of his world? She had not yet noticed him standing behind her; her attention seemed focused on the pond. He really should not engage her, but an impulse too strong to ignore urged him forward. She drew him like a desert moth to a flame-spider's glowing web, one tentative step at a time.

The bubbling sound of the fountain reached his ear, finally coming to life for no apparent reason. And bird song. Not a lot, but there were clear chirps emanating from the tall, droopy tree on the pond's opposite shore.

His attention was riveted on the sprays of tiny white

flowers woven into the female's brown...what *was* that on top of her head? Not headfeathers, obviously. Whatever the soft-looking strands of silk were called, they were elegantly swept up into some kind of fastener. Something deep inside him stirred, a strange aching around his heart that all but stole his breath.

Who is *she?*

He must see her face. Must hear her voice. Must touch her, because all that would be enough to explain why he was here in this place with her.

He reached out one hand toward the graceful curve of her shoulder.

The soft intake of her breath echoed in his ears, and she straightened as if she had sensed him.

"Who's there?" Her whispered words were odd, foreign, yet he understood.

He stopped, frozen by indecision. Should he touch her, or wait for her to turn around? She was already turning her head, the soft curve of her jaw holding his gaze, a breath away from revealing her face....

"Kai Firewing."

The garden, pond, and female snapped out of existence, replaced by the familiar sands of the Bezchian desert. And the beloved presence of Fya Firewing, his first mentor and Most Esteemed Elder of his youth. The mother-figure who had found her soul mate nearly two hundred sun migrations ago, and left the clan to join him as a mortal.

Fya smiled. "Hello, Kai."

"F-Fya?"

She presented as she had been the last time he had seen

her: young, around twenty-seven sun migrations. Her brilliant red headfeathers curled up at the nape of her neck, and her equally red wings arched high behind her.

"Forgive me for pulling you out of your first dreamwalk, but there was no choice. My time is limited and there are things you must know."

"I…how are you *here*?" He squeezed his eyes shut tight, then opened them again. She was still there, hands in the pockets of her baggy purple leggings—the ones shot through with silver threads—and her torso covered by her favorite white flying leathers. "This is not possible. You left the clan two lifetimes ago."

"Aye, I assure you it is possible. You just have not learned the art of timeslipping yet."

So this place was not real, only an image of the shifting dunes of home.

Fya drew one hand from her pocket and tucked it into the crook of his arm. "Come. Walk with me, my brother."

All he could do was abide by her request and fall into step with her slow, meandering pace. "You risk timeslipping from the past to speak with *me*?"

That was something phoenixes did not learn to do until they were eight or nine hundred sun migrations. It took a lot of energy and focus. And if he was not mistaken, she was projecting herself from two hundred sun migrations in the past.

"Of course." She said it as if it was no great feat, but it was. Timeslipping took several lifetimes to learn.

"I am humbled." He frowned down at the sand. "But, why would you do this?"

6

"To be blunt, there is change coming, and you, my youngling, will be at the center of the storm."

That sounded dire. Especially when he had spent his life trying to stay out of storms, both real and figurative. But timeslipping…amazing. When in the throes of matching mates, all phoenixes could see the shadows of the couple's possible futures, which was why their services were so highly valued. But Fya had been a clear-seer. She could see all possible visions of the future exactly as they would play out if they happened. For *anyone*, not just her matching assignments.

Obviously she had seen his future, and deemed it concerning enough to risk a timeslip.

He swallowed against the growing knot of apprehension lodged in his throat. "What did you see?"

"Great happiness, or devastating loss." She met his gaze, and there was no duplicity in her golden eyes. Only concern. "I know that sounds evasive, but the final outcome depends upon which of your destinies you accept. I cannot tell you what you should do, but I can warn you that the future of our beloved Bezchi rests on your choices."

The urge to burrow into the sand and hide from the emotional repercussions of her declaration enticed his internal empath. "Is *that* all?"

"Aye. All I can tell you without influencing your freedom of choice, anyway."

"Why did you not tell me this before you left our colony?" That would have been a simpler, and safer, plan.

She stopped and faced him. "Have you forgotten how poorly you reacted when you learned I had met my soul mate, Avok?"

Shame burned his cheeks, and he lowered his gaze to stare at his toes. "I have not forgotten."

Her departure to become mortal had driven him into an immature rage. Avok Rockdweller, a male who he had never met, would take his most beloved family member to her death. She would lose everything, give up her very life to be with him. It was so final to one so long-lived.

Fya cupped his cheek, a gesture he had once thought he would never experience again. "You were a youngling."

"It was my second younglinghood. I should have known better."

"Yet you behaved as one of only six sun migrations should. And that is all right." Her soft sigh had the same echoing quality as the whispered words of the unknown female from his vision. Or dreamwalk, if Fya was correct. "Even though we retain our memories from rebirth to rebirth, our bodies and minds do react age-appropriately, most of the time. I will never hold your actions from then against you, Kai."

He caught her hand between his. "I did not want you to die." *Still wish you had not.*

"I know." The truth of her words shimmered in her eyes.

"And, I am very sorry for making your departure harder, and less joyful, than it should have been."

"I know that too." Her smile widened. "Last thing, before Most Esteemed Elder Uri interrupts us...the female in your dreamwalk is—"

"*Kyzel Raptorclaw did* what?"

Most Esteemed Elder Uri's angry shout jerked Kai from the timeslip, and the reality of the meditation garden crashed back firmly around him. He grabbed the edges of the stone perch and flared his wings out to keep from toppling over. As with an older body of any species, falling from even a small height was not without risk of injury.

What in the howling winds was the most esteemed elder fuming about now?

Kai tilted his head to one side, but no more angry words came from Uri's white adobe nest on the far side of the meditation garden. The whisper of the hot breeze through the pyre fronds once more filled the air, unchallenged, as it should be.

Whatever the problem was, it was unlikely to involve him. No one would want to risk further embarrassment to the Firewing clan by asking for his help.

He rotated his shoulders and shook the tension from his wings. Like Fya, Uri was a strong leader for the clan, the eldest of the elders—one thousand migrations around the sun—which was a long time to live. Could it be that living that long made a bird crankier?

I hope not. He scrunched his nose. The mere thought was unbiddable.

"The female in your dreamwalk is...."

Is what? If only Uri had not interrupted before Fya finished her sentence. Was the unknown stranger—clearly an off-worlder—connected to his life-path? If so, it would have helped if she had turned completely and revealed her face. All he knew for certain was she was female, had brown head-silk, and was not Bezchian.

And what about the rest of Fya's message? It sounded like

9

he could be a harbinger of change. A shudder went through his wings.

As if being an outcast is not enough.

A flash of topaz drew his attention to the thumbnail-sized fire-beetle climbing along the patagium of his wing. A quick finger-flick sent the insect tumbling through the air, the sunlight catching its faceted shell in rotating glints before it landed in an ember-berry bush.

Kai studied his wing feathers. The frosty silver of age seemed heavier on his secondaries than his primaries now—the much-loved deep garnet red of his wings in his youths all but gone. The body of this incarnation must be too old to be a part of the change to which Fya eluded. Perhaps he would have an early rebirth? That would hopefully reset his mate-matching abilities, even if he came out of regeneration early instead of going all the way back to infan—

"*El-der Kai.*" Uri's voice cracked through the peace, again.

Kai jerked his head around. "Yes, Most Esteemed?"

Uri leaned out an open window of the adobe structure, his brilliant red feather cap catching the sun's light in a glittering array around his head. "Attend me, please."

"Aye, Most Esteemed."

He lowered his feet over the edge of the meditation perch until he found the ground. Ah, the bliss of curling his toes into the warm sand. He heaved himself up to stand, flexed his wings, extending and retracting the stiffness out of them, then gave them a shake back into place. One of the downsides of aging: his body seemed to respond less and less favorably to prolonged periods of inactivity.

He approached the red gossamer veils of the entrance to Uri's nest, the sand shifting and churning under the soles of his feet. The memory of lacey white flowers against soft brown head-silk rose up, and he stopped. Who *was* she? And why would he walk through the dreams of a female he had never met? A female who had stirred the most unusual, and pleasant, feelings inside him. Breathless feelings without names. Ones he had never experienced with any female before.

Of course, all the females he knew were phoenixes, like him. His sisters. And they were in no way breath-stealing.

He gave his head a sharp shake and scrunched his face into a scowl. If he dreamwalked with her again, he would pay closer attention to discern who she was, and where she might live.

For now, his leader awaited him. He stepped into the cool main room of Uri's nest, and inhaled the sweet-musky scent of the sacred *cinbin* spice. The room was long, narrow, and sparsely furnished. To the right, a handful of straddle-perches, arranged in a circle for casual seating, sat atop a woven mat over the rough-rock floor. To the left, a chest-high table surrounded by ten tall perches with crimson cushions dominated the dining/meeting area. Long, wooden storage chests lined the walls at various intervals on both sides.

"There you are, Kai." Uri paced from one end of the room to the other. "The situation is intolerable."

The most esteemed elder was a mere thirty sun migrations into his current incarnation, and moved with the natural fluidity of his physical age.

Kai glided deeper into the room, toward the meeting table, savoring the gentle abrasiveness of the coarse stones against the bottoms of his feet. "What situation, Most Esteemed?"

"The monarch of the Raptorclaw clan." Uri stopped pacing and turned his golden-eyed gaze toward him. The color was more common in their kind than Kai's own dark purple. "Someone should clip his wings."

"You mean, Kyzel Raptorclaw?" The most rational and dependable monarch of all the Bezchian clans.

"Yes. Yes." Uri fluffed his wings in agitation, something he rarely did. Whatever had happened had deeply unsettled the eldest elder.

"What has he done, Most Esteemed?" *And of all the elders, why would you speak to* me *about the situation?*

Uri compressed his mouth so tight his lips nearly disappeared, and his eyes widened far enough that they appeared about to pop out of their sockets. This *was* bad.

"He shunned the Elders and left Bezchi two days ago to seek a mate from...*Earth*." A visible shiver rustled through Uri's wings.

"*No.*" Kai reached out a hand, closing his fingers around the smooth edge of the wooden table.

Had Kyzel Raptorclaw been gripped by the mindlessness? It was rare that the cognitive-stealing disease occurred in someone of barely sixty sun migrations, yet it could happen. Although, the surviving monarch of the Raptorclaw clan had seemed perfectly rational at his mate's funeral a sun migration ago.

Still, there was no guarantee. The mindlessness was an

exceedingly slow disease, giving the victim and their loved ones several sun migrations to plan and prepare. And in Monarch Kyzel's case, he would have stepped down immediately so a new monarch pair could be elected.

"Sadly, yes." Uri resumed his pacing. "The situation is unacceptable...and dangerous. If he is successful, more Bezchians could turn to this...this...*agency* for mates. It could spell the end of our ancient tradition of matching mates. This cannot be allowed. Traditions are put in place for reasons."

"What agency?"

"The Silverstar Agency." Uri smacked his fist into his palm. The crack of skin meeting skin snapped through the room. "They match older Earthlings with beings of like age from other worlds, and have a stellar reputation for success."

The Earthlings practiced mate-matching? Kai shook his head. Well, why not? Many other worlds did, but none had dared encroach on Bezchian tradition.

Uri raised his still-clenched fist. "They *must* be stopped. We must determine Raptorclaw's intentions."

"You suspect he has an agenda?"

"I do not suspect; I am certain. Over the last several of sun migrations, he has pressed hard to convince the clans to back his idea of opening up trade relations with Earth. Once they agreed, his prime advisor, Rol Raptorclaw successfully managed to arrange the negotiations." The most esteemed narrowed his eyes. "I fear this new move is a way to undermine the elders' authority."

"But why would he want to do that?" Kai slammed his lips back together, but it was too late. The question was out.

"Why?" Uri's face was almost as red as his headfeathers. "*Why*? If I had the answer, then I would not have to send you to Earth to investigate."

And, there it was. The reason he was here. "Would it not be better to send a physically younger elder?"

Uri peered at him through narrowed eyes. "Have you had any of the signs of rebirth? Hot flashes? Cold shivers? Cravings for *cinbin*? Urges to nest?"

"No."

"Pah." Uri waved a hand as if in dismissal. "You have never rebirthed before your hundredth sun migration anyway."

"But, why me? Should not another with a better matching record be honored with this duty?"

Uri drew himself up, his eyes flashing with condemnation. "Are you questioning me, Kai?"

"Forgive me, Most Esteemed." Kai pressed his palms together and bowed from the waist. "I know I have been a disappointment most of this incarnation, but I promise not to fail you, or our clan, in this duty."

It was a big promise, but this was an opportunity to restore his reputation, so naturally he would fully dedicate himself to the task.

"Good." Uri nodded, apparently satisfied. "Now, go prepare yourself for your journey. You will need a portable deep-space communicator, as I will expect regular updates. We must know more about Raptorclaw's intentions, and put an end to this plan of his to take an off-worlder as a mate.

"Also, if the Silverstar Agency is the threat I suspect, they must be stopped before other clans turn to them for their mates. The trip to Earth takes two days. A transport will depart from the dock an hour before sundown, so you have just enough time to have a universal translator implanted." Uri made a shooing motion with his hands. "Go now. Go, go, go."

"Aye, Most Esteemed." He hustled back out into the afternoon sunshine.

It seemed a bit farfetched that Kyzel Raptorclaw intended to ruin the Firewing clan, but the most esteemed's concern was not without merit. The monarch's behavior did seem odd.

TWO

Nixy Vogel stared at the Silverstar Agency's application on her computer screen—*her* application. The one that'd been a simple test to see how her employer's most recent version worked—because that was what a responsible agent did for her clients. She'd done this every single time there was an update, and never, ever, had her faux applications been mysteriously sucked into the system. There one moment, then—*pow!*—gone the next. And it'd been in there for seven stinking months now.

Dammit, dammit, dammit.

She finger-punched the delete key on her keyboard with rapid-fire precision.

Ding.

Ding.

Ding.

The monitor screen blinked with each error chime filling her tiny living room.

"Why won't you just *delete*?" There were a thousand

better ways to spend a Saturday, but here she was once again, futilely wrestling with technology.

She fought back another wave of impending doom. The one hard and fast rule of the agency was: employees are prohibited from submitting personal applications. No exceptions. This was going to cost her her job. Eight years of stellar service notwithstanding. Sure, it was an accident, but how could she prove it?

I should have gone to Jordan immediately.

But she hadn't. She'd been so sure she could handle it herself. What her supervisor didn't know wouldn't hurt her. Nixy pursed her lips into a pucker. Should she be relieved or disappointed that no match had been found?

A small stress-laugh escaped her. Wow. Her brain had actually gone *there*? Not having found a match was literally the least of her concerns. Besides, she'd already met the love of her life...and lost him. She let her gaze drift to the eight-by-ten frame on her fire place mantle. The one of her and Efrem on their wedding day, ten long years ago. Efrem tall, slim, and handsome in his black tux, with a head full of salt and pepper curls, and her in a lacey, ivory tea length dress, with baby's breath woven into her brown hair.

A huff of dry humor escaped her. Brown hair that'd gotten too gray over the years, until she'd caved and colored it a reddish-purple. On Efrem, gray had looked distinguished. On her, not so much.

She brushed one straight, blunt-cut strand back behind her ear. Her memories of the three years they'd had together had been enough to keep her going so far. And it looked like those memories would be all she had after Jordan fired her.

Reality check, Nix: you're not the first agent to have broken that rule.

She was just the only one who hadn't been caught. Yet. It was only a matter of time. How could her supervisor have missed this?

Good thing I used my full name, not my nickname.

That was the only logical reason she hadn't been busted already. *Nixy* would have definitely caught Jordan's attention.

A strange tingle blossomed at the base of her skull, as if something exciting was about to happen. It spread like goosebumps down her arms and over her breasts. Damn, even her nipples stood at attention, visible through her T-shirt. Had a ghost touched her, or something?

She swept the living room with her gaze. Everything seemed normal…the well-padded couch, end tables, lamps, built-in bookcases. "Efrem?"

Silence, except for the laughter of the neighbor's kids playing next door. But still, the feeling lingered. She gave her head a shake. It didn't *feel* like Efrem, and besides, he only ever appeared to her when she revisited their wedding day at the winery in her dreams.

You're spending too much time inside alone again.

An easy thing for a fifty-five-year-old widow to do.

Ping.

She glanced at her cell phone on the side table and grinned at the text on the screen.

Opal Lentz: Tea?

Goodness, her elderly neighbor had the best timing. It was such an unlikely friendship, but Mrs. Lentz had shown up at her door shortly after Efrem's passing, bearing the gifts of understanding and the bond of widowhood.

Nixy picked up the phone and thumb-texted back—a skill she'd managed to teach herself despite having fat thumbs.

Nixy Vogel: Yes! Bringing shortbread.

Thank goodness Mrs. Lentz had agreed to installing a friendship gate between their backyards. Made it easier to visit.

Opal Lentz: The girls are out. Close the gate.

Ah, so the chickens were free-ranging in Mrs. Lentz's backyard. Cute little fluff-bonnets.

Nixy Vogel: Will do. See U in 5.

She flipped the lid of her laptop closed, set it aside with the phone, and pushed out of the easy chair. Tea was just the thing she needed to distract herself from work woes and weird feelings of anticipation.

A smaller shiver went through her. What in the world would make her feel like that anyway?

Kai floated on Earth's air currents toward a boxy building built on the right angles of a street corner. Earth was unexpectedly delightful. At least, the desert site of the galactic spaceport was. The small city where the Silverstar offices and guest residences were located was situated on the other side of a small mountain range, closer to the coast, and therefore somewhat cooler. Still within an acceptable temperate range, though.

He alighted on the roof, and adjusted the pack attached to his flying leathers. Then he squatted to run his hand over the closely cropped blades of greenery covering the landing area. The plant struck a familiar chord, a memory he could not quite grasp. He had seen something similar somewhere before, but how was that possible?

In all likelihood, it was nothing important. What he needed was an entrance to the building. Monarch Kyzel was purported to be residing on the top floor of this five-storey building, so it should not take much time to find him.

Kai scanned the rooftop. There; that glassed in archway must the access point. He rose and strode toward it. The glass double doors parted even though there was no obvious sensor visible.

He stepped through the doorway into an open space large enough to comfortably fit at least a dozen phoenixes. Frigid air surrounded him, sending a shiver down his spine and through his wings. It was as cold as winter in the mountains where part of the Rockdweller clan lived. And as barren. Just some potted plants, a tall counter, and another pair of double doors—in silver-green brushed metal, not glass. Almost the exact color as the leaves of the cinbin bush back home.

"Welcome to Silverstar. Can I help you?" The question came from a young, wingless female seated on a tall perch behind the counter.

"Aye." His gaze fell on a meter-tall metal piece affixed to the wall next to the metal doors behind the female. "What is that?"

She glanced over her shoulder, revealing a tiny device plugged into her ear, partially hidden under her straight blonde head-silk. "That's the letter 'R' in the English alphabet. R for roof."

So, it was a letter? Why had his visual translator not recognized this? He gave the implant behind his ear a sharp tap, then focused on the letter again. An almost imperceptible click came from the implant, followed by recognition of the letter.

He breathed out a soft sigh of relief, then turned his attention back to the female. "I must go to the fifth floor."

"You need an appointment with one of our agents before you can access the residential floors."

"Why? I am here to see Monarch Kyzel Raptorclaw, who resides on the fifth floor of this building."

"What's your name?"

He straightened with self-importance. "I am Elder Kai Firewing."

Surely now that she knew he was from the revered clan of mate-matchers, she would grant him access.

"Okay, hold on a sec." She tapped her finger against the ear device. "Adam, there's a visitor up here for Monarch Raptorclaw.... Elder Kai Firewing.... Okay, thanks." She tapped it again and met his gaze. "Adam will be right up to help you."

"Can you not take me to the monarch?"

"No, I'm sorry." She smiled in a friendly way. "I'm stuck behind this desk until my shift ends. But he'll only be a couple minutes."

"Is that a long time?"

"Um, no?"

Good. "I will wait."

It would probably be advantageous to learn how time worked on Earth, even though he should not be here long enough for it to matter. He had even packed lightly: a few changes of clothing and the portable deep-space communication device.

The silence in the space lengthened, and still no *Adam* appeared. Kai pursed his lips. If left to his own devices, he would have located Raptorclaw by now.

Ding.

The chime was followed by the soft swish of the silver-green doors opening. A slim, wingless male stepped out of the box-like room behind the doors. "Elevator hold."

Human clothing varied widely, it seemed. The workers at the spaceport had been attired in loose dark-blue one-piece uniforms. The female behind the desk wore a short-sleeve white top with tiny round fasteners running down the front, and dark gray leggings with crisp, vertical creases.

This male, however, had a different style. His fitted long-sleeved shirt hinted at sinewy muscles underneath. And the black leggings, made of a thick fabric, hugged his legs, ending in narrow openings around his ankles that seemed too small for his feet to fit through.

The female stood up as the newcomer strode forward. "Thanks, Adam."

"Sure thing, Steph. Hello, Elder Kai, I'm Adam Rosse." Everything about the human was friendly, from his smile to his brown eyes. Even the sandy streaks through his light brown head-silk hinted at a relaxed personality. "Lucky thing I decided to come in today. I'm usually not here on Saturdays. Unfortunately, Monarch Kyzel isn't in right now, but his advisor cleared you to come to their suite. We can take the elevator down."

Not much of what he said made sense, except the part about Kyzel. "What is an *elevator*?"

"It's a transportation contraption that gets us from floor to floor." Adam beckoned him forward with a hand wave. "The entire building was designed to comfortably accommodate even the largest of the Alliance's species. Step this way."

Kai, following the younger male, stepped into the windowless box-room.

"I presume this is your first time on an Earth elevator, Elder Kai?"

"Aye."

"Then I recommend you hold onto the bar at the back." Adam pushed a round button directly under the one marked with an *R*. For roof. "It's not fast or anything, but it might be disconcerting if you're not used to it."

This was all very strange, but Kai shrugged and wrapped his hand around the silver bar attached the back wall. The doors slid closed, and the sensation of downward movement pressed against his body.

He met Adam's gaze. "This is like an Alliance lift."

"Yup."

Ding.

The doors opened to reveal a long, wide corridor.

"This way." Adam stepped off the lift and strode forward, and Kai followed. "The building is 'L' shaped. The lower two floors are Silverstar Agency offices, and the upper three are residential units, called suites, where our clients—and sometimes their guests—stay. This floor is reserved for winged clients, so they can access the roof."

"If an 'L' is the same as a right angle, then I understand."
Adam chuckled. "Close enough. Here we are."

The door was as wide as the ones on the roof, and
matched the coloring of the elevator doors. The only thing
differentiating it from the lift were the head-high symbols
"5-A" in silver. Adam tapped his knuckles against it, and it
opened with a swoosh.

Just inside stood the imposing figure of Rol Raptorclaw,
prime advisor to the Raptorclaw monarch. Most of the clan
were large, like him, but Kai had had enough dealings with
them over his lifetimes to not be intimidated.

Rol nodded. "Elder Kai."

"Prime Advisor Rol." Kai stepped into the spacious
common room. "I am sorry to intrude, but I must speak with
Monarch Raptorclaw."

"He is not here."

Kai puckered his mouth in distaste. "So I heard. When is
he expected to return?"

"Later tonight." Rol shrugged his massive shoulders.
"You may wait here, if you wish. We have an extra room if
you need it."

Adam cleared his throat. "If you're all okay here, I'm
going back to my office."

"We are fine," Rol replied. "Thank you, Mr. Rosse."

The door slid shut and Rol turned away. "Make yourself
comfortable, Elder."

"Thank you." He fumbled with his pack's straps,
disengaging it from his flying leathers then dropping it on
the floor next to the back wall. "It has been a long trip."

"I understand." Rol sat on one of the four tall, backless

perches around the eating table. "Please, take a perch, Elder. We have not seen you since Careene's funeral. Have you been well?"

"Well enough." He slid onto the perch directly across the table from the prime advisor. "I am eager to speak with Kyzel, though. Where is he?"

"He is spending the day with the female he has been matched with by the agency." Rol gazed down at the tabletop with a frown.

This was not the news he wanted to hear, but there was a small, suspicious tick in Rol's jaw that indicated he too was not entirely pleased with the situation.

Kai studied the other male. "You do not approve of his choices."

Rol shot him a narrow-eyed glare. "He does what he believes is best for our clan, and for Bezchi."

"But he is breaking with tradition."

"He has the clan's approval." The raptor looked back down at the table. "And mine."

"Of course." He opened himself up to sense Rol's feelings.

Duty struggled against a tide of discord. The clan's approval or not, Rol was a traditionalist in conflict. His reluctance to talk about it made it clear he was torn between supporting his monarch and his own personal beliefs. The monarch's prime advisor could be the key to ending the match before it was too late, and that would please Uri to the upper atmosphere and beyond.

As long as Monarch Kyzel was absent, it would be easy to stir Rol's doubts until he was primed for subtle suggestion and took action. There was, after all, no hiding emotions from an empath. Something Rol should know well.

Kai folded his arms atop the table and leaned casually against them. "Once a monarch breaks with tradition, then others will follow."

Rol raised his head and locked gazes with him. "Perhaps the elder would like a refreshing glass of *lemonade*?"

Raptorclaw practically flew off his perch and headed for another wide arched doorway behind Kai. Oh, yes, a nerve had been struck. A little more agitation should work to get the prime advisor to take action.

The sound of glassware tinking together came from the room Rol had entered. Kai folded his hands atop the table. Patience was easy for someone as long-lived as him. Everything happened in due time, in his experience.

A few moments later, the prime advisor plunked down a glass of pale-yellow liquid in front of him. "Lemonade."

"Thank you." He raised the glass to his lips and took a cautious sip. The tart-sweet flavor flowed over his tongue like a beverage from the Great Aerie itself. How could such deliciousness have been created by a race of ground-bound beings?

He swallowed, lowered the glass, and smacked his lips a couple of times. "That is quite…refreshing, as you said."

Rol shrugged, sipping from his own glass. Not the talkative sort, that much was clear. No matter.

Kai took another larger gulp, then set his glass on the table. "You are aware that you are in the position to save our culture from such a devastating collapse."

A hint of doubt slipped through Rol's agitation, a sure indicator that his words were getting through.

Rol curled his lip in a silent snarl and jutted his chin in the direction of a different archway, this one set in the back wall. "The bedrooms are through there. You may use the second one on the left."

He stood abruptly, and stomped away down the same hallway, presumably to his own quarters.

Ah, the seeds of doubt had been planted. Give him time, and Rol could be an effective means of bringing the rogue monarch to heel.

A quiver of unease churned through his stomach, and he frowned at the glass between his palms. He had done the right thing, certainly. Must just be the lemonade not settling well.

THREE

Another Monday, and still Nixy's problem hadn't disappeared in a puff of magic over the weekend. She draped her sweater over a hanger and place it on the closet rod. *Wishes won't wash dishes.*

She closed the closet door and turned to face her office. Mornings were the best time of day, with sunlight pouring through the row of windows of her second-story office. She slipped into her chair behind the antique wooden desk, opened a little white paper sack, and drew out the yummy butter croissant within.

Despite her more eclectic cottage-clutter decorating style at home, the minimalist look worked better for her here. The desk—a wedding gift from Efrem—dominated this end of the room. Four client chairs of different designs—because not all off worlders could sit in human chairs—were arranged in front of the desk. And a row of low cabinets lined the inside wall.

She broke off a flakey piece of the croissant and popped it into her mouth. That spark of joy this place brought her was as strong as ever. How lucky she'd been to land a job with the Silverstar Agency, and to have had the chance to work her way up to being a placement agent.

A soft knock drew her attention to the sliding double doors set into the office's inner wall. "Come in."

The door slid open far enough to admit her assistant, Adam Rosse before it slid closed again. "Kyzel Raptorclaw is here to see you, if you're free."

So, the winged monarch of Bezchi had finally returned from his weekend with Robyn Martin Donahue. This had to be a good sign. "Send him in, please, Adam."

"He has a *guest*."

"Is it Ms. Donahue, by any chance?" She allowed herself a little smile of satisfaction. Those two were as good as married. Or mated. Whatever the Bezchians called it.

"No. It's the Bezchian elder I told you about, who arrived on Saturday."

That sensation at the base of her skull tingled back to life, and she drew in a quick breath. If she were the full-blown superstitious type, she'd suspect something big or important was about to happen to her. Like her life was about to change, which was ridiculous. She was too old and too set in her ways, and completely happy about it.

And besides, she was only slightly superstitious. "Okay. Go ahead and send them in."

"Sure thing. Be right back." Adam slipped back out, leaving her alone again—for the moment at least.

The young man was the best assistant she'd ever had. Like a son. And, he hadn't called her ma'am since the first day he'd been hired, after she'd oh-so-gently reamed him a new one for using the "m" word.

She gave her head a shake and refocused her thoughts. So, Kyzel was here, accompanied not by his prime advisor or his bodyguard, but an *elder*? Sounded important. Could be a new potential client, in which case it was first-impression time.

She made a quick visual inventory of her desk. Computer monitor off, pens in place, croissant crumbs—she smoothed her hand over the cool glass surface that protected the wood—swept into her palm and into the trash. Okay, now she was ready to make a good first impression on this mysterious Bezchian elder.

The door swooshed open, all the way this time, and Adam walked in, followed closely by nearly seven feet of grinning royalty. That was what she liked to see—happy clients. Meant she was doing her job right, and that counted for something. Everything, actually.

She opened her mouth to greet him, but her gaze was snagged by the shorter, somewhat older—yet still impressive—Bezchian entering in the monarch's wake. He was golden-skinned and gorgeous, with elongated eyes and pupils so dark they could be as black as his loose leggings. The red of his flying leathers complimented the silver sheen of his wings and headfeathers. Her fingers twitched in response to her completely inappropriate desire to explore those glorious wings.

A wave of heat washed over her, and it was all she could do to not hand-fan her face. What a lousy time to be hit with a hot flash. Good God. She was losing all professionalism, but who could blame her? He might not have the stature of Kyzel or the two members of Kyzel's royal entourage, Rol and Fyad, but he was still over six feet tall—and easily the best looking of the bunch.

Also the oldest, a solid fifteen years older than her, give or take a year or two.

Geez, woman, you're getting all hot and bothered by the guy. Throttle it back.

She cleared her throat and made to stand up, only she wasn't seated anymore. How had that happened? *When* had that happened? Why didn't she remember getting out of her chair?

"Good morning, Ms. Vogel." Kyzel's warm greeting was a welcome anchor point.

"Monarch Kyzel, how are you today? How are things going with Ms. Donahue?" *Please introduce me to your friend.*

It didn't seem possible, but the guy's smile got wider. "Very, *very* well. We will be spending the upcoming weekend together. Robyn calls it a weekend getaway."

"That's wonderful." Come to think of it, she'd never made a client match for off-worlder royalty before. Kind of cool if it all worked out, and there didn't seem to be a reason it wouldn't.

Kyzel nodded his head toward the handsome Bezchian now standing beside him. Finally. "This is Elder Kai Firewing. He arrived over the weekend and asked to meet with you."

"Me?" She shifted her gaze to Kai, and caught a faint whiff of cinnamon.

Kai straightened and raised his chin slightly as if trying to look down his nose at her. "I am an *elder* of Bezchi, and I make mate matches among my people."

Oh good, something they had in common. She gave him a smile. "Sounds a lot like what I do."

"Not exactly." He enunciated every syllable.

Huh. Someone seemed full of himself. Strike one.

"Mind your tone, Elder Kai," Kyzel said, then turned his attention back to her. "He is hoping to talk to you about evaluating the similarities and differences between your respective roles and duties—if you have the time, of course."

There was a pleading look in the monarch's eyes, as if he'd found himself saddled with a relative visiting unannounced. Well, she could appreciate that.

"Sure. I can spare about fifteen minutes."

Kai looked up at Kyzel. "Is that long?"

Kyzel said something too low for her to catch, and the elder nodded. "Aye, this is acceptable."

The "aye" was kind of cute, but the attitude had to go. "All right. Adam could you get us some refreshments, please? Have you ever tried iced-tea, Elder Kai?"

Kai's expression turned hopeful. "Is that like lemonade?"

"Uh, no. But you can have a wedge of lemon in it, if you'd like."

"I believe I would like."

"Great. Monarch, will you join us?"

Kyzel shook his head. "I have things to see to. Even in my absence, I still have duties to my clan. I will send Fyad to retrieve Elder Kai at the end of your session."

Which meant she would be entertaining Kai alone. This could be a good thing.

Kai watched Adam lead Monarch Kyzel out of the room, heard him promise to return shortly with the *iced tea*, but it all seemed distant. As if he was a spectator viewing the scene from afar.

It had been that way since he had entered Nixy Vogel's spacious office, met her brown-eyed gaze, and a hot flame burst to life in his chest and curled around his heart. Was this some new symptom of impending rebirth? And if so, why had it happened the moment he walked into her presence?

"Won't you have a seat, Mr. Firewing."

"*Elder* Kai." The correction seemed juvenile, even to him.

"Sorry." She brushed a strand of her straight, reddish-purple head-silk—or *hair*, in her language—back behind her ear, and an unfamiliar, yet pleasant, floral scent wafted past him. "Elder Kai."

For a female of such short stature, she had a vibrant presence. The silky fabric of her white blouse draped over the soft mounds of her ample breasts. A bold red fabric flower was pinned high on her top, which dared to distract him. He lowered his gaze down to where her hand was propped at the waist of her hip-hugging straight black skirt. The desk blocked the rest of his view, but this female was in charge, and knew it. And that appealed to him in a way he did not wish to examine too closely.

He forced his gaze away from her and straddled the Bezchian-style perch. Her office was a comfortable room, built to easily accommodate even a Bezchian as large as Kyzel. Wide, with very little furniture aside from a well-proportioned wooden desk, a long cabinet that ran the length of the inner wall from the door to the corner, and four perches of varying sizes and styles. Wise choices when providing a service to the different body types her clients must have. Almost reminiscent of Uri's main room.

Plenty of natural light flowed in through the windows lining the outer wall. All in all, an efficient and cheerful work environment.

"Well, now." She sat down. "Do you want to start with questions?"

He had plenty of questions, like, why was her hair the color of a desert sunset? Why did she wear a red flower? Did she live nearby? Where were her other personal effects, besides the small picture frame atop her desk? The one turned away from him. Did she have a family? Was she mated?

No!

He did not need or want to know the answer to that question. Or any of them, for that matter. He was here for a reason, and if he did not stay focused on that reason, the most esteemed elder would bind his wings until his rebirth.

"Tell me your process of matching beings together." There, that was a good opening statement. Clear, to the point, and not easily avoided.

She raised her thin eyebrows at him. "Well, I can tell you that the process is thorough."

She dared be evasive? "Do you ever have failed matches?"

"Of course we do. But only a tiny fraction, compared to other dating agencies." She leaned forward, her breasts pressing against her folded arms. "You must have failed matches too, from time to time."

"Rarely." The sour taste of the lie rose at the back of his mouth.

Failed matches were part of the reason he had come: to vindicate himself. To prove he could succeed at an assignment—any assignment, not just matching. To be respected again as a vital contributor to clan and colony.

She grinned. "Obviously, we are both very good at our jobs."

Oh, yes, he had been good, at one time. And if she loved her job half as much as he loved his, she would also do anything to protect it.

A pang of guilt poked at his belly. He needed information from her, anything to help complete his mission to stop the royal match and discredit the company for which she worked. But she seemed unwilling to give it to him.

Perhaps Rol was resolving the problem even now. The prime advisor had departed the travelers' nest moments after Kyzel returned this morning from his two-night romp with *that human.* Although, there was no guarantee of the prime advisor's intentions. It was probably better to charm Ms. Vogel, get her to feel more comfortable in his company, until she revealed the secrets of Silverstar. Not as equals, of course...that could never happen. But certainly as colleagues—to a degree.

He gave her what he hoped would be perceived as a disarming smile. "I cannot imagine doing anything else."

"Really?" Her expression was as warm as the midday sun, and her breasts still rested over her arms, enticing his gaze—but he must remain *focused*. "Me too. How long have you been matching, erm, mates?"

Was that a question he could answer? *Should* answer? The average mortal lifespan on most planets was one hundred sun migrations, or *years* in her language. But not so for the Firewing clan. There was no way to know how she would react to that revelation. How much danger would it be to the clan if he told her the truth about his almost infinite lifespan?

It was not worth the risk. "I have been joining mated pairs all my life."

"Wow. All your life? When did you figure out that's what you wanted to do? I didn't figure it out until I was in my mid-forties, after…." Was that a flash of pain in her brown eyes? "After I, um, grew up."

What was this? Was there more than one secret she was keeping? And why did the idea of discovering her secrets intrigue him so?

He tilted his head to one side. "After a big event in your life, Nixy Vogel?"

She stared at him, as if weighing her response. Oh, yes, something had happened to bring her to Silverstar.

She shrugged her shoulders. "Yeah, you could say that. Anyway, how about you? Twenties? Thirties?"

"*All* my life." A little candor could not hurt. It might lull her into revealing more. "Members of the Firewing clan begin training from infancy."

Her mouth opened with the slightest pop, a sound that stirred the most pleasant shiver down his arms and through his wings. "Your parents allowed that?"

Focus on her words, fool.

He cleared his throat. "I do not know my life-givers."

"How could you *not* know—ohh." She slapped her hand over her mouth. "I'm sorry. I didn't think that through. You were adopted?"

"In a manner of speaking. We do not normally speak of this to outsiders." And for good reason. In this case, however, he had no compunctions about dangling that morsel in front of her.

"Sorry. I'll shut up now."

No, please do not. He must keep her talking, if for no other reason than to hear the gentle notes of her voice. "It is good you found an occupation that makes you happy. It does make you happy, correct?"

Why would he even care? But, for some reason, her happiness was important. It made no sense.

"Very happy." She met his gaze again, and a fresh wave of heat coursed through his veins.

"What did you do before this?" What was it about her that intrigued him so?

"I was an accountant." A bubble of laughter came from her, strangely bittersweet. "I put big numbers in little boxes for a finance company. Balancing the books every month was rewarding, but not as exciting compared to this."

What an odd job: putting numbers in boxes. "Connecting mates is exciting. The feeling that fills me the moment I match a pair is unlike anything else."

Only the joining of a phoenix with their soul mate pairing was better—or so he had been told. But that meant mortality and, eventually, final death. Despite Fya's eagerness to join with her soul mate, the mere thought of permanent death disturbed him. At least he was still far too young to have to worry about that happening. Most phoenixes were a thousand sun migrations or older before they met their soul mate.

"Yes, *exactly*." A spark of energy flashed in Nixy's eyes and her excitement plunged into his heart, even though he had not opened himself to her emotions. "I love it when a couple I've introduced tells me they're getting married...or mated. I've only had two couples not work out so far. Both made me sad."

"Ah, yes, I agree." He must regain control, refocus himself on his goal of rooting out useable information. He shifted on the perch, folding his arms over the top of the chest rest. "How do you know who to introduce an applicant to?"

She glanced at the computer monitor on her desk. "Oh, well...." Her gaze snapped back to him and she narrowed her eyes. "That's something I only discuss with clients, Elder Firewing."

Pah. He had almost had an answer. "So, you will not share?"

"No, of course not. It's company policy."

He pushed himself off the perch to stand. "Then we have nothing more to discuss."

Her eyes widened, as if she was surprised. "I...I guess not."

"Good day to you, Ms. Vogel." He gave her a curt nod. "I will find my own way out."

"O-kaay."

The office door opened before he reached it, and Adam stepped in carrying a tray. "Iced tea's here…um…. Too late?"

Kai glared down his nose at the youngling. "I am sure Ms. Vogel will enjoy her refreshment more without me."

He stepped around the human male and strode out of the office. This was not the end of it, though. Not by a long flight. He would get the information from her eventually, then begin undermining the agency's process. The only thing standing in his way…besides Ms. Vogel…was exactly how to complete his task.

Poor Adam looked so bewildered by Elder Kai's abrupt departure. The young man turned a confused gaze on her. "Was it something I said?"

Nixy expelled a small chuckle. "He's a prickly one, for sure. But don't worry, it wasn't you. It was all me. Come on in and have some iced tea with me, Adam."

It wasn't the first time they'd shared a break together. Adam carried the tray to her desk and busied himself with setting up. "Want to talk about it?"

"He's up to something, I can just feel it." She reached for the tall, narrow glass Adam handed to her, the surface slick and cool under her fingers. "He seemed awfully interested in our vetting process."

There was no telling why, but the urge to resist that question had felt like the right decision.

"You mean he was awfully interested in *you*." Adam wore a smug expression as he took the seat across the desk from her. "I mean, the Punjabi-style pants are nice, but they're not the ass-huggers the Raptorclaw guys wear."

She raised her eyebrows at him. "Oh, stop."

And here she'd thought it'd just been her libido out of whack. But, before Kai had left in a snit, she'd been feeling the same vibes.

Adam grinned wickedly over the rim of his glass.

"Oh, for God's sake, Adam, did you *see* him? He's way too old." And no matter what her body said, she wasn't keen on being widowed again.

"Say what you will, I saw how that guy looked at you. And you at him."

Wow, that hit a little too close to the mark. "Hey, let's change the subject, shall we?"

"Because you know I'm right?"

"How about you? Got a special girl...or guy...in your life yet?" Adam had never hidden that part of himself from her, and she treasured his confidence.

It wasn't that being bisexual, or any part of LGBTQ, meant what it once did on Earth. The advent of first contact with the Alliance had led to many positive changes. But still, there were some hold outs on the subject, and some unions were outright banned. Namely groups of more than two.

A flicker of surprise flashed in his eyes, then was gone. "Not yet, *Mom*."

"Well? What are you waiting for?"

"For you to retire." He raised his brows and one corner of his mouth rose in a smug half-grin, then he took a sip of his tea.

This time a full-on laugh burst out of her. "You're going to be waiting a long time then, my friend." Or not, depending on when Jordan figured out her little transgression.

"I know." Adam's grin took on an affectionate curve. "I wouldn't have it any other way."

FOUR

One week later.

Storms and lightning, the situation as *outrageous*. Kai paced the length of the travelers' nest's common room. In the week since he had parted Ms. Vogel's company, she had turned down all his requests for another meeting. But then, thank the eternal ones, Kyzel's human match, Robyn Martin Donahue had refused to mate with him. Everything had been settled, and Kai had been eager to return home, victorious, with Raptorclaw's entourage.

That was when it all fell apart. The sedate departure from the galactic spaceport two days ago had blown up into a fiasco when Rol—*Rol*—had flown Ms. Donahue in just moments before the ship had been scheduled to depart. And she had left with Kyzel to be his mate, and the newest monarch of the Raptorclaw clan, while he, Kai, had remained on Earth, searching for a way to stop the Silverstar Agency from destroying his clan.

The gum in his feathers was that only he knew the *true* reason Kyzel and Robyn were together.

He stopped and gripped the seat of one of the tall perches, or stools, as the Earthlings in this region called them. "How? How are they *love mates*?"

Love. What a shock it had been to discover that this was the *exact* element that had been missing from all those matches he had botched. Love was the only explanation for the wave of bright, shimmering warmth that had radiated from the pair. Like the birth of a new star. That sort of connection was exceedingly rare, to the point of myth. No one on Bezchi was mated for *love*.

Mating is not *about love.*

A surge of wrongness lurched through his belly at the thought. It must be a mistake. That glorious feeling he had picked up from Kyzel and Robyn must be nothing more than his imagination.

But, would it not be wonderous if all matches were this way?

"Pah." This went against everything he believed.

He must remember his mission. He had already failed to stop Kyzel from mating, but he would not fail in stopping the Silverstar Agency from stealing away any more Bezchians. The incident at the spaceport was no more than a fluke, not even worth a second thought.

The swoosh of the front door opening drew his attention to the two beings entering the travelers' nest.

Or, more specifically, Fyad dragging a human female inside.

"Oh, good." The female raised her chin. "A witness to my kidnapping."

Fyad stopped. Surprise and guilt flashed in his black eyes. "Elder Kai. I did not realize you would be here. Is this not the normal time for your daily fly-about?"

Kai moved his gaze between Kyzel's black-winged bodyguard and the female dressed mostly in black. A warm effervescent lightness, like soaring on the air currents of a spring morning in the desert, swept through him.

Love mates.

Again.

How is this even possible?

"Elder?"

It could not be. He gave his head a shake. Absolutely could not be.

The female frowned. "Is he okay?"

Fyad nodded. "Sometimes his kind go into trances."

This was not a trance. He had simply been stunned into immobility. Which, it could be argued, was almost the same thing.

"They can do that standing up?" The female peered at him like he was an interesting artifact worthy of closer scrutiny.

"Standing, sitting, flying, wherever they happen to be. If he collapsed or burst into flames, that would be a problem. But this," Fyad waved one hand in his general direction, "is normal."

The female's mouth fell open. "Burst into flames? This sounds like a great story."

"Can you stop being a reporter for longer than three minutes, Ms. Crawford?"

"Nope." She placed her fists on her hips and glared up at

Fyad. "And it's Raven. I think that abducting a girl off the beach puts us on a first name basis."

Kai managed to open his mouth. "I am not in danger."

Amazing that he had managed to croak out a string of words that made sense.

Both of the younglings relaxed, then Fyad tugged the female's hand. "We still need to talk, *Raven*."

"No shit, Sherlock."

"My name is Fyad, not Sherlock."

"Funny. I thought it was Shit-for-brains."

They passed Kai and headed into the corridor leading to the suite's private quarters—their bickering trailing behind them.

Two love-mated mixed pairs...that was unprecedented. Inconceivable. Unless this divine, yet inexplicable, sensation of rightness actually was a new symptom of impending rebirth.

Stop letting yourself be distracted.

He curled his fingers into fists. Ms. Vogel *must* have done something to influence the younglings. Yes, yes. It was time for a new strategy to stop the Silverstar Agency before anymore Bezchians fell prey to their service. But, how? Ms. Vogel refused to share how the agency matched their clients. It had something to do with her computer, though. She had glanced at it when he had asked. She had also alluded to other matching agencies, like Silverstar, on Earth. Maybe, just maybe, they would be more willing to share their processes.

Aye, that might work. Rol had proven to be unreliable in his mission. Even now, the prime advisor was meeting with the female Silverstar had matched him with. It would be just his luck that they too would be love mates.

A dry laugh escaped Kai and he resumed his pacing. First order of business was to find privacy, a place to do his research without the potential of interruptions or questions from Rol. It would mean leaving this travelers' nest and finding a new one. There were other types of travelers' nests on Earth called *hotels*—that much he had learned since his arrival. All he had to do was figure out where they were located, and which ones accepted Alliance currency. Then he would find a way to slip away without the prime advisor finding out.

A cold shiver ran up Kai's spine and through his wings. It would be nice if he could retire to the meditation garden at home right now. Soak up the comforting rays of the sun as he formulated his plan.

"Raise common room temperature twenty Bezchian degrees." If he could not be home, then at least he could be warm and comfortable.

FIVE

The sound of a commotion drifted from the lobby area through the open office door. Nixy raised her head and frowned. What in the world was going on out there?

"*Ms. Vogel.*"

Her heart rate accelerated at the sound of a man's voice. *Kai's* voice. He hadn't gone back to Bezchi with Kyzel and Robyn after all. So where had he been the last few days?

Kai strode into her office followed closely by Adam, who, being all of five feet ten inches, looked like an angry cocker spaniel chasing a Doberman.

"I told him he wasn't welcome...."

Kai came to a stop by the client chairs in front of her desk. "I will speak with *you*, Ms. Nixy Vogel."

Adam insinuated himself between her and Kai. "You'll have to go through me."

Kai blinked and looked down, as though just realizing Adam was there. Then the vertical creases across his forehead deepened on either side of the widow's peak created by his headfeathers. The Bezchian equivalent of raising eyebrows.

Oh, boy. Time to step in. "Adam, it's okay. I'll talk to him."

Adam shot an incredulous look at her from over his shoulder. "You sure?"

"Yes, I'm sure." She made a shooing motion. "I'll buzz you if I need anything."

Adam sighed and retreated, glaring at Kai until the office doors swished closed.

"So, Elder Kai, what can I do for you?" Shame on her for not asking him to have a seat, but really, she didn't want him getting *too* comfortable.

Yes, you do.

No, you don't.

Oh, boy, now she was arguing with herself.

He closed the final few steps between himself and her desk. "I have done many hours of research, and have concluded that several other Earth-based match-making companies use *applications* to bring their clients together."

There was that cinnamon scent again, setting her mouth to watering. She swallowed. "Good to know the computer in the suite is getting some use."

"I moved to a hotel yesterday."

Now why would he do that? Not that she cared…she didn't. Right?

Kai narrowed his eyes at her. "Through this manner of data collection, one person can get *several* suggestions for potential matches."

"Some people like variety." That wasn't Silverstar's

M.O., though, which was why the additional DNA requirement had been effected.

"They do not even *attempt* to provide a valid mate." He slammed one fist against her desk, and the photo of her and Efrem rattled. "This is insulting, degrading. They mock the necessity of bringing two beings together in a match that benefits both their flocks."

"I suppose…." She hadn't really thought of it from that angle before.

"Is this how you process your clients, Ms. Vogel? With an *application*?" He spat the word like it was something foul.

Wow, he seemed over-the-top offended. "Why do you want to know?"

"I want to know how many other so-called matches you had for Monarch Kyzel."

"That is none of your business." The answer was zero, but like hell would she tell him.

Her gaze was drawn to the little tick of his jaw. A sudden urge to kiss it until it stopped twitching rose.

"Why do you refuse to answer my questions?" He ground out the words as sheer frustration flowed from him in waves.

Because I have a sneaking suspicion you wouldn't use the information for good.

If she'd learned anything in her five-plus decades, it was to trust her gut.

He braced his fists on her desk and leaned close. "*I* know why. Because your agency is a fraud. *You* are a fraud, Ms. Vogel."

Oh, now wait a gosh-darn minute. "You know what? I am so done with you. Get *out*."

Was he paler than he had been a second ago?

"No." He swayed a bit, then recovered his balance.

No?

She opened her mouth, but no words came out. How dare he? Kissable jaw twitch or not, this had gone on long enough.

"All right then." She gripped her armrests, pushed out of her chair, and strode toward the coat closet in the corner.

A moment later, she emerged with the fire extinguisher.

He drew himself upright with a haughty frown. "What is that?"

"*Out.*" She pulled the trigger, and a gust of chemical fire retardant blasted in the direction of his sandaled feet with a loud whoosh.

He retreated a few steps, drawing one wing around himself for protection. "How dare—"

Whoosh.

This time he made it to the door before turning. "I will—"

Whoosh.

She followed him out to the lobby, past a wide-eyed Adam, as Kai sprinted into the elevator leaving a trail of foam footprints across the floor. The doors opened immediately to his frantic pounding of the call button, and slid closed behind him with a soft thump.

Blessed silence settled through the disheveled waiting area.

Adam stared at her, mouth open and eyes alight as if she were some sort of Amazonian queen. His shoulders quivered and a sound rumbled in his chest, then exploded out of him and he doubled over with laughter. Her own laughter bubbled out, but sounded somewhat hollow to her ears.

"Well." Adam swiped a knuckle under each eye. "The cleaning crew won't be happy, but that's one way to get rid of a nuisance."

"True." Kai had been a nuisance.

Adorable, but still a nuisance. What was his problem, anyway? And had she really been contemplating kissing the jaw of someone who had such a low opinion of her—and the agency?

Even so, it still didn't sit right that she had chased him out like a stray dog.

Kai curled his hand over his belly as he staggered into the penthouse hotel suite, his wings dragging across the marble floor behind him as if weighted down by rocks. Rebirth had many symptoms, but feeling physically ill was not one of them. Thank the eternal ones Fyad had ignored his order to remain here. There was no telling where he would be if the youngling had not followed him to the Silverstar building.

Another round of needle-sharp jabs tore at his gut and a groan welled up. "Need to...lay down."

"Allow me to help you to the couch, Elder."

"No...bed." Kai leaned fully into the bodyguard's side. "Over-extended...myself...this afternoon."

He had been fine until he had called Nixy a fraud. That had been when the first pains shot through him, but there was no reasonable explanation as to why.

Fyad grunted and changed trajectory toward the bedroom door.

"Fyad." Kai wrapped his fingers around the youngling's wrist. "Do not fret. Not rebirth symptoms, only exhaustion. I will be better in the morning."

"If you say so, Elder." Fyad's black eyes were full of concern and doubt.

Nothing he could say would ease the bodyguard's misgivings now. "I do say so, and best you remember. I am the elder."

Fyad smiled as he eased Kai face-down on the bed. "I will not forget. Sleep well, Elder."

"Aye." He breathed out the word on a sigh as exhaustion creeped over him like a dark blanket.

If only he had not been so harsh to Nixy….

The garden was familiar, lush in its floral laden greenery. *Roses.* Kai ran a finger over the velvety softness of the brilliant red petals. And the springy green turf under his feet was *grass.* He knew that now. This was an Earth garden, and so different from the meditation garden back home.

He bent and inhaled through his nose, but no scent came from these roses. It was as if they were soulless images of their real-life counterparts.

A sweet instrumental melody floated on the sun-lit air, calling to him, urging him forward to find its source. He moved with reverence between the rose bushes. It was odd that his feet made no sound, even though he clearly heard the music. It all had a dream-like quality, but why would he dream of a place he had never been before?

A soft sob reached his ear. It seemed that not everything in this place was right. Such a shame to be sad in this beautiful setting. He pushed on, rounding the final bush. A short distance away, a long white runner was staked down to the grass, and white human perches with backs were set up in rows on either side.

Off to the right was a pond…. A memory broke loose. He *had* been here before, that's why it was familiar. The pond, the fountain, the tree with the drooping branches. But the chairs and runner were new this time. And so was the tall white arch, covered with the palest pink rosebuds imaginable, at the opposite end of the runner.

Odd that everything beyond the arch was fuzzy. It appeared to be rows of some sort of tall-standing vines. A crop, perhaps?

What is this place?

It appeared like a very special event was set to happen here. But the only person he could see was an Earth female standing at the beginning of the white runner with her back to him. Same lacy dress, same upswept brown head-silk, same tiny white flowers…she must be the same female from his dreamwalk.

That is it. I am in another dreamwalk.

And dreamwalks did not happen without a reason. It was up to him to ascertain that reason.

The female drew in a ragged breath and her shoulders shook. It was her crying he had heard. An overwhelming urge to comfort her filled him. He stepped closer, reached out, and touched his fingers to her shoulder.

The female drew in a sharp breath and turned toward him. "Who...wha.... *Kai*?"

"*Nixy*?" But not the Nixy he knew.

This wide-eyed woman was a younger version, and slimmer, though still full in all the right places. And tears streaked down her face.

"You look...you look...different." She shook her head. "Younger. Like you're in your mid-forties."

He did? He raised both his hands and turned them back and forth. They did appear less wrinkled and gnarled than normal. How odd.

Nixy snorted. "Just figures."

He returned his attention to her. "What do you mean?"

"That you'd invade the happiest day of my life."

"Forgive me," he lowered his hands to his side, "but how can this be the happiest day of your life if you are crying?"

She stared at him as if his wings had just fallen off, then huffed. "Oh, what the hell, why not? It's just a dream, right?"

"Aye." He jutted his chin in the direction of the chairs. "Would you explain what is happening here?"

"Yeah." She sniffled. "This was my wedding day."

Disappointment clenched at his gut. "Wedding? You mean mating?"

She had a mate? That knowledge should be a relief, yet he grappled with an emotion he had rarely encountered in his many sun migrations: jealousy.

"Yep." She turned her attention toward the archway. "And that's my husband, Efrem."

Kai followed her line of vision. The chairs were now full of fuzzy images of humans, and under the arch stood two human males. One of them was a blur of black, but the other was clear. "The tall one, with the…facial silk?"

"It's called a beard." Her smile was wistful as she stared at the slim male dressed in a black suit. Silver threaded through his curly hair and *beard*. "Yeah, that's him."

There was undeniable sadness in her gaze, and Kai's heart ached for her. The empath in him yearned to take her pain away so the lively sparkle would return to her eyes.

"Tell me about him." He waved his hand to include the gathered group. "About them."

She met his gaze, as though surprised by his offer to listen. Truthfully, it baffled him as well, but the gesture was natural—dream or not. *Her* dream. Which he had been drawn into, again.

A thought niggled at him, as if he should know why this was happening, but it flitted away the moment he tried to grasp it. It would come back when the time was right. Thoughts like that always did.

Nixy shrugged her lace-covered shoulders. "Guess I do need to talk about it, even if it isn't for real. C'mon."

There was no choice but to follow her as she stepped onto the white runner and pointed to a weathered, but grinning, white-haired female dressed in vivid blue. "That's Aunt Eden, she taught me how to cook. Then there's my Uncle Ned, who was like my second father."

As she named them, each relation and friend became clear for a moment before fading back into the gathering. So, those who were most important to her were the only ones he would see, the ones she bore deep fondness toward.

"And this is Efrem." She came to a stop in front of the male, her gaze full of love.

Efrem smiled down at her and cupped his hand over her cheek. "I love you, Nixy."

A twinge of pain poked at Kai's heart and he drew in a sharp breath. What was this jealousy toward a male he had never met?

This is not the first time I have felt this way toward a stranger.

But, this time it was different than his resentment of Fya's mate. This time there was a possessive edge to it he could not explain.

"Are you okay, Kai?"

"Fine." He rubbed his hand over his chest, which did nothing to relieve the ache. "How long have you been mated?"

"Together for three years, married for two." She returned her attention to Efrem. "Then he was diagnosed with prostate cancer. I lost him four months later."

"He is…."

"Dead." She met his gaze. "It's been ten years."

Waves of sadness rolled over him. Her sadness. Her loss. Her sorrow. And he opened himself to it, took it, accepted it as if it were his own.

Nixy's gasp cut through the emotional tidal wave. "What's happening to me?"

She took a jerking step toward him, and he reached out and drew her into his embrace. There was no logic about his action other than that this was what an empath did if they chose. Taking her emotions, giving her a respite, was as natural as breathing for him. Even though this was a dream.

The urge to fold his wings around her was strong, but that might scare her. And it would shut out Efrem. He raised his gaze, and Nixy's mate met it as if he could see Kai. But that was not possible, was it? This was a dreamwalk. Yet there was no denying the intense awareness in the other male's brown eyes.

Efrem's mouth curled into a small smile and he nodded as he faded, then dissipated like a morning mist.

Something profound had just occurred that defied explanation.

Nixy tipped her head back and he met her gaze. "I...I don't understand, but I suddenly feel at peace. Like everything just clicked into place."

"An undeniable rightness." With a female who was his rival in the waking world.

One who would never let him hold her like this outside of a dream. Ah, but what was a dream other than a wish? And at this moment, he wished desperately to kiss her— something he would never do in reality.

He lowered his head and breathed out her name. "Nixy."

Her lips parted, and her soft brown eyes reflected his desire. It was the approval he had hoped for. He brushed his lips over hers gently, in case she changed her mind, then sealed his mouth to hers, taking her sweet breath and stroking her tongue with his.

Fire raced through his veins, just as it had the first time he had seen her. It consumed him, consumed his soul.

Crack!

Blackness spun around him, tearing him from her embrace and sending his body careening into nothingness like an out-of-control fledgling in a storm.

Nixy startled awake with a shout of surprise. Her heart slammed like it would burst out of her chest any moment as the flaming heat that scorched her insides cooled by slow degrees. The sound of her ragged panting filled the pre-dawn semi-darkness of her room.

Same old dream, but this time….

"What…the *hell*?"

Kai had been there. How had…no, *why* had she dreamed of him? She pressed her fingertips to her lips. It'd felt so…real. That kiss had done things to her, given her feelings that still resonated even though she was now awake.

Feelings for Kai. Feelings she liked.

She swallowed hard against a knot of uncertainty lodged in her throat. "It was a dream. Just a dream."

But, holy moly, what a dream. Talking to Kai, telling him about her marriage, the gentle nudge from behind that had sent her stumbling into his arms….

"*Efrem!*"

She scrabbled sideways, reaching for the lamp switch and giving it a twist. A soft white light filled her room, enough to see the framed photo of her and Efrem in Yosemite.

"You *pushed* me. Why did you push me? I mean, it'd be one thing if he was Chris Evans or…or…what's his name—

Axill Lund, that guy from the Cosmos Warriors movies. Sexy guys who haven't been jerks toward me. But Kai Firehouse, or whatever his name is? Efrem, *really?*"

Aaaand she was shouting at a photograph. A long groan escaped her and she flopped back against her pillows. "Geez, Nix, get it together."

Adam would laugh at her, if he knew. Which he wouldn't ever, because she wasn't sharing this with anyone.

She glanced at the clock. Four thirty-nine, and she had to get up at six. No point in trying to go back to sleep now, especially since there was a chance Kai might make a reappearance in her dreams. She wasn't ready to deal with him again just yet.

She reached for the photo and ran her fingertip over Efrem's smiling face. "God, I miss you."

There should be a stabbing sorrow in her heart right now, but it was suspiciously absent. Instead, there was something new there that she couldn't name. But it wasn't negative, or painful.

The sensation of Kai's strong arms around her, the skin of his warm, bare chest under her cheek, surrounded her as if the dream hadn't completely faded.

She gave her head a sharp shake of denial. "I don't have *time* for this."

More like, she didn't want to examine the new emotion too closely. She pressed her lips to the cool glass covering the photograph, then set the frame back on her nightstand.

Time to stop thinking about that and get ready for the day.

SIX

After assuring Fyad he was feeling much better, and would not explode into flames this morning or anytime soon, Kai retreated to his room and pulled the portable deep-space communicator out of the dresser drawer. Contacting Uri with an update now could be disastrous, but the most esteemed expected to hear from him daily.

I do not have *to mention the dream.*

But, he should. Uri had the uncanny ability to detect untruths. Possibly even from lightyears away over a communicator, although Kai had no personal experience with that.

He set the flat white box on top of the desk. It did not take up much space, considering it was as long as his forearm and just a bit thicker than his thumb. Alliance tech had come far in the last three hundred sun migrations.

Now was the best time to make contact. Fyad was out by the hotel's swimming pool, brooding over not having seen that human reporter love mate of his for a few days. Why the two of them could not seem to see their bond for what it was,

was mind boggling. Had to be because one of them was not Bezchian.

Ping.

Kai's gut tensed. Uri had beat him to requesting the call. Time to bury his unsettling feelings for Nixy and make his report. He waved his hand over the surface of the device, and Uri's miniature image flickered into existence atop the communicator.

"Greetings, Most Esteemed Elder."

"Greetings, Elder Kai." The projection and the audio were clear and interference-free. There would be no cutting this call short due to a poor connection. "I await your report. What progress have you made?"

Keep as close to the truth as possible.

"Progress is slow. Yesterday, Ms. Vogel forcibly removed me from her office." *Please do not ask how.*

"It sounds like slow does not convey the true extent of the situation. Nonexistent might be a better word, yes?"

Probably so. But, if Uri believed that, he might cut the mission short and order him home. The image of Nixy's fiercely determined expression rose up, then was quickly replaced by the haunted, sorrowful younger version from her dream. Fulfilling his duty was not the only reason he wished to stay on Earth—for a little longer at least.

"No, not in this case." He ran his tongue over his lips then swallowed. "I have reason to believe my persistence is wearing her down."

"This is good." Uri did sound approving. "It would be best to have her unwitting cooperation soon. Monarch Kyzel and…*Monarch* Robyn have arrived, and many are lauding their relationship as the strongest match ever witnessed."

How quickly Uri's approval had turned to a grimace of disgust.

"I am sorry for allowing the situation to get out of wing, Most Esteemed. There is a tradition here on Earth of giving flowers when attempting to solicit a female's favor. I will start with that to soothe Ms. Vogel's emotions and win her trust."

"They give *plants* to each other?" There was an edge of surprised disbelief in Uri's tone.

"Not the plants, just the flowers cut from the plants." It was a strange custom. "Then they gather them into a grouping called a *bouquet*."

"But, the flowers will die."

"Yes, I know, but—"

"*Kai.*" Uri's impatient tone cut of his words.

All the muscles between his wings tensed, and he braced for the words sure to follow. "Aye?"

"Just see it done." Uri's projection disappeared, the communication disconnected from the most esteemed's end.

Uri had not ordered him home. He must still trust him enough to get the job done.

Kai relaxed his wings. "Aye, Most Esteemed."

Nixy slapped her palms against the surface of her desk. Dear God in heaven, why was she *still* thinking about Kai's dream kiss last night? The guy was a grade-A jerk, and it was unbelievable that she had actually dreamed about him.

It was also unbelievable that Efrem had nudged her into Kai's arms. And that kiss—because, of course she couldn't string together two thoughts without going back to that—if he could kiss in real life the way he dream kissed, then whoa, Nelly, she was in trouble.

But that wasn't going to happen again, no sir. Not in *her* dreams, and definitely not in real life. What she needed was a good distraction.

Ring.

Her cell phone trilled from its charging post next to her wedding picture.

"Ask and ye shall receive."

She peered at the screen. Jordan Jones, her supervisor. A hard, tight knot formed in her chest and she cast a guilty glance at the computer. Jordan *knew*. And now she was calling to bust her butt.

Ring.

Argh, she had to pick it up—get it over with. Deep breath, in through the nose…she sucked in a deep breath…and out through the mouth. She released it in a measured gust through her pursed lips.

Ring.

There's no escaping the inevitable.

She gave the speaker a finger tap. "Nixy Vogel."

Please don't let Jordan hear that little quaver in my voice.

"Hi, Nixy." Jordan's tone was brisk and businesslike. "A small issue has come to my attention. I'll be in town on Tuesday, and would like to stop by to discuss it with you."

"Um, okay. Anything I should know beforehand?" Even a hint would be helpful.

"No, and it's not urgent. We just need to talk."

Not urgent could be good. Or it could mean that Jordan didn't want to fire her today and ruin her weekend.

"All right, what time?"

"I have meetings most of the day, so sometime in the afternoon. Would four work for you?"

Nixy brought up her calendar. "Yes, four works."

"Good. See you then." The phone made the short ping of a disconnected call.

Tuesday. Four days—three and a half, actually—before she might lose her job. She leaned back in her chair. "I wish I'd learned how to be an IT guru."

Beep.

Now what? She gave her office phone a sidelong look. Whew, it was just Adam.

She gave the phone a finger tap. "Yes, Adam?"

"Batten down the hatches, we have an incoming Bezchian."

"Elder Kai?" There went her heart again, beating a little faster.

"Yep. He just entered the elevator on the ground floor. Should I send him packing?"

Say yes. "No."

Ooh, what was she doing?

"No?" Even Adam sounded surprised.

She released a small sigh. "I'll see him."

Because really, could her day get any worse?

Kai clutched the bouquet in front of his chest. It was a useless protection against Adam's narrow-eyed glare, but having it between him and Nixy's tenacious assistant did give him a sense of comfort.

Adam waved his hand in the direction of Nixy's office door. "She says you can go in."

Cautious relief seeped in. Her approval was no guarantee she would be receptive to his words, but it was a start. "Thank you."

Adam made a noncommittal grunt and returned his attention to the computer monitor on his desk. A disdainful dismissal in any language.

Kai approached the doors and they slid open.

"Hey."

He turned back to Adam and gave the male a questioning look.

"Fire extinguisher," Adam murmured, and raised his eyebrows pointedly. "Behave."

"I intend to." The future of his world depended upon him getting on her good side. So, no more antagonizing the pretty Silverstar agent.

The swish of the door closing behind him cut off Adam's scowl, and Kai turned his attention to the female standing behind the desk at the opposite end of the room.

Nixy. *Real* Nixy, not the younger dream Nixy. The familiar feeling of his blood turning molten blasted through him at the sight of this more mature, beautiful version. Or maybe it was an incredibly intense pre-rebirth hot flash.

"Hello, Elder Kai." Her tone was as cool as a high mountain breeze just before the first snowfall.

He cringed inwardly. Yes, he deserved that sort of welcome for how he had treated her. And more so for what he had to do.

"Good day, Ms. Vogel."

She raised her eyebrows. "I trust we aren't going to have a repeat of your last visit."

The fire extinguisher, or the dream kiss? He swallowed the impertinent question back down. She did not need to know that it was really him in her dreams.

"I was out of sorts yesterday and handled the situation poorly." He closed the distance between them as her gaze flicked from his face to the flowers and back. "I am hopeful that we can put my past mistakes aside and start anew."

He came to a halt in front of her desk and extended the bouquet, six bright yellow *sun flowers*. Their name alone made them a worthy gift.

The corners of her mouth twitched as though she was fighting a smile. "Is this a peace offering?"

"If that is what keeps you from chasing me out again." He gave her what he hoped was a sincere enough grin. "I am very sorry for my words. It was not my intention to hurt you. You are in no way a sham, Ms. Vogel."

The truth of his words wrapped around his heart, and her brilliant smile gave it wings. Utterly the opposite effect from his hurtful words during his previous visit.

"All right," she said. "I accept your apology, *if* you forgive me for using the fire extinguisher on you."

"It is forgiven, though I did deserve it."

Her laugh was like the bubbling fountain in the meditation garden back home, soothing and joyful. He transferred the gift into her hands. The brush of her fingers against his ignited another wave of fire, and he clamped down on the urge to react with a full-body jolt. Her soft intake of a breath drew his attention to her slightly parted lips. Would the red paint on them make them taste different than they had last night in the dream?

And why in all the heavens was he thinking about kissing her in reality? Only soul mates were attracted to each other in such a way. She was simply a means to an end.

"I'll find a vase for them later." Nixy set the flowers on the desk next to her phone and cleared her throat. "Won't you have a seat, Elder Kai?"

The pink blush on her cheeks was lovely, and she smelled like Earth roses. He blinked twice, three times. What was happening to him? This female was human, therefore not a match for him.

But, what if…?

No, it could never be. Phoenixes soul mated with other Bezchians, not off-worlders. He straddled the nearest perch and settled himself onto the cushioned seat as he folded his wings close to his back.

"Now," Nixy said. "What can I do for you, Elder—"

"Kai. Just Kai."

She tipped her head the tiniest bit to one side, then nodded. "Kai."

That was so much better. "I…."

He what? Now that he was here, his mission seemed ridiculous. Selfish. "I was hoping to…get to know you better, Ms. Vogel. I believe there is much we have in common."

Where did that *come from?*

Nixy stared at him as though contemplating his worthiness. Then she leaned forward, arms folded on the edge of her desk. "First, it's Nixy, not Ms. Vogel. Second, can I take you to dinner tomorrow night…Kai?"

The way her breasts rested on her arms was an art form…wait a minute. What did she just say?

He dragged his gaze back to hers. "D-dinner?"

A chance to speak with her on more neutral territory?

The pink on her cheeks deepened and she sat back, clearly flustered. "Sorry. Sorry. I didn't mean—"

"Aye."

She froze in place like cornered prey. "Y-you will?"

"Aye." And he truly meant it, as surprising as that seemed even to him. "I would be honored to share a meal with you."

Her smile slowly came back. "Well, good. How about I meet you downstairs outside the front doors?"

"Of course. I propose we defer our discussion until then."

"Oh, sure." She waved one hand in the direction of her computer. "That's a good idea. I just got in a dozen new applications today, so I'll be working late to get them processed."

"In that case," he rose from the perch. "I will see you tomorrow evening."

"Sounds good."

Somehow her positive reaction buoyed his heart as he strode toward the door.

"Kai?"

He stopped and turned partway around as the door swooshed open. "Yes?"

"Do you like spicy foods?"

"Very much. I also eat meat." What had possessed him to add that?

"Okay." She waggled her fingers at him. "Bye."

"Bye." He stepped through the doorway into the reception area.

Adam looked up from his desk. "Looks like all went well. No shouting. No fire extinguishers."

"Aye, as I promised." He pressed the button for the elevator. "Did you think I would break my word?"

"Let's just say, I wasn't a hundred percent convinced."

A chime sounded and the elevator door opened.

"I see." Kai stepped into the transportation box, turned, and locked his gaze on Adam's. "Nixy invited me to dinner tomorrow night."

There was something immensely satisfying about the way the door closed on the male's stunned, wide-eyed expression.

SEVEN

---*---

Same park, same lawn, same arch, but something had changed. Every time Nixy had escaped into this dream, it had been a refuge, a place to revisit her past, see Efrem again.

But this time Efrem wasn't there and everything else seemed to be made out of tissue paper. One sprinkle of rain would set the colors running in rivulets until it all melted away. Including the grass she sat on.

I want to hear the birds sing.

The gentle coo of a mourning dove reached her ear. And somewhere beyond the empty archway, where the rows of grapevines normally stood, came the muted chatter of chickadees, or finches, or some sort of flittering small bird. But it all lacked the clarity of before. She leaned forward to rest her arms on her drawn-up knees.

What's wrong with me?

"There is nothing wrong with you, Nixy."

She closed her eyes and allowed herself a relieved smile at the sound of Kai's deep voice. "I knew you would come."

Or, at least, she'd hoped he would. It was kind of nice not to have to wait until their date to see him again.

"Did you?" He stepped up next to her and lowered himself to sit on the ground, then stretched out his wings to each side so they partially rested on the grass, one directly behind her. "The white runner and rows of chairs are gone."

"And the guests, and the vineyard." Why did she dream of him with flaming red wings and headfeathers?

"Yet the rose bushes remain."

She glanced behind her. "Yes, they do." With blooms as red as his wings. "The pond too."

Her gaze skittered to the golden skin of his bare chest. A sinewy strength projected from him, even in real life. Human guys his age weren't built like that, but human men also didn't need to stay in shape in order to fly. That alone would be a motivator for anyone. And, to be honest, she rather liked Kai's sleek muscular structure over the bulkier bodies of Kyzel and the others she'd met from the Raptorclaw clan.

Geez, what was wrong with her? Sure, this was a dream, but gawking at him still seemed invasive. She lowered her gaze to study the way the light fabric of his orange harem pant-like leggings settled against his muscular legs. It was too bad he was so much older in real life.

Why'd I ask him out on a date, then?

She sighed and forced herself to look out over the pond. It wasn't a *date* exactly, just two colleagues getting together for dinner. That was all it could be, right? The most they could ever be was friends. She'd already found the love of her life, and that lightning bolt didn't strike twice.

"Where is Efrem, Nixy?"

An invisible claw closed around her stomach. "I…I can't find him." Or he didn't want to be found. He *had* bumped her into Kai's arms during the last dream, after all. "He was a good man, y'know."

Kind, sweet, supportive…everything she had waited to find in a husband.

"Aye, I believe that. You would not put up with an unworthy mate."

Darn right. "I miss him."

"I know. I can feel your sorrow."

He could? She looked up into his eyes. "Are you an empath or something?"

"Aye." He nodded, the dream sunlight shimmering over his headfeathers. "It is important to honor what he stood for, but not at the cost of living."

Wow, this was great. Her very own dream psychoanalyst to help her through the stages of grief.

Hey, whatever works.

She was hardly in a position to complain. "That makes a lot of sense, Kai." Why couldn't he be more like this in real life? "Do the birds sound louder to you all of a sudden?"

"Look over there." He pointed toward the arch, but it was what was beyond the arch that grabbed her attention.

"The *vineyard* is back. But where are the chairs, and the runner?" And the guests, and the priest?

And Efrem?

"Those are part of the past now." He met her gaze. "But the rest of the universe still surrounds you and is very much alive."

A spark of defiance tried to catch in her heart. "Well, the arch is still here."

"And it always will be." Kai brushed a strand of her hair back behind her ear. "As it should."

His words settled around her like a warm, fuzzy blanket on a cold day. Everything was as it should be, all of it. "Efrem isn't really gone, is he?"

Kai shook his head. "He will always be a part of you. Part of your past." He touched his finger to her chest directly over her heart. "Right here."

A sense of excitement bloomed over her skin from that touch point, spreading like goosebumps until it encompassed her entire body. Everything was okay. *She* was okay. And, somehow, Efrem's absence didn't feel hollow anymore.

"You are a good soul, too, Nixy Vogel. Do not ever doubt that."

"I'll try not to."

She scooted closer to Kai, leaned against his side, and rested her head on his shoulder. After a moment, the soft rustle of feathers reached her ear, and his wing appeared over her shoulder, curving around her. She allowed her eyes to close, and the bird song to fill her until it too faded away as sleep claimed her.

EIGHT

Kai strode into the living room area of the penthouse, the sand-color silk of his leggings swishing pleasantly around his legs. "I will be going to meet Ms. Vogel now."

Fyad turned away from whatever he had been staring at outside the panoramic windows, and frowned. "I advise covering yourself with a *nayar*, Elder."

Kai frowned and looked down at his chest, bare except for his red flying leathers. "I see no problem."

"As Monarch Kyzel discovered, human females seem to appreciate a suitably clothed male. At least, when going to dinner."

"They do?" This was news to him.

"Very much. And Monarch Robyn once claimed to prefer Monarch Kyzel's light blue nayar because it matched his eyes."

How interesting. "I do have one in dark purple."

"That would work well." Fyad nodded, a gleam of approval in his eyes.

Purple it was, then. "Thank you for your advice, Fyad. I shall go cover myself."

Never in all his lives had he considered dressing to match his eyes. But, if Nixy might like it, then why not?

I am not supposed to care.

Yet, there was something agreeable about being appealing to her—*for* her.

I have a mission to complete.

Worms of descent squirmed in his belly as he reentered his bedroom. It was wrong to play with her emotions, but how else could he get the information he needed to protect the ancient traditions of the Firewing clan? What a quandary. Perhaps he was not the phoenix for the job after all.

I dare to question the most esteemed's orders?

Uri was wise, had many hundreds of sun migrations of experience and knowledge. Had the welfare of Bezchi in his heart. Knew things Kai had not yet learned. And then there was the matter of earning back the honor of being a phoenix. Had he not failed his clan enough?

He waved his hand over the closet door sensor and the maroon panels parted. Uri and the clan were lightyears away. Tonight, he would wear purple. For Nixy. What could one time hurt, especially if it lowered her guard?

He quickly draped the nayar over his head and laced up the sides. Then he hurried back to the living room.

"I am ready."

"Very good, Elder." Fyad indicated at the door with one hand. "I will remain out of sight."

What a pain in the wing that the bodyguard insisted upon going, but the youngling did have his orders—as he had made abundantly clear the day Kai had attempted to sneak away from the Silverstar suite. "Aye, then, let us go."

The Silverstar building was only a three-minute fly from the hotel. They entered through the rooftop access and took the elevator down. Kai exited the front doors alone the same moment Nixy approached the building, a vision in her red dress.

Her color choice could be intentional, or not. Either way, the dress hugged her voluptuous curves, stopping at her knees. The matte black shoes on her feet had tall sticks attached to the heels, which gave her extra height and accentuated the beautiful shape of her calves.

If red had not already been his color of preference, it certainly was now.

He brought his gaze back up to her breasts, round and full. A tremor ran through his hands in response to his inexplicable desire to touch her there. This was the behavior of one who had never seen a beautiful female before, which was not true in his case. Many of the females he had met had been quite lovely, but had never captured his attention. Ever. No female would except his soul mate. His body was for her and her alone, because that was how it always happened.

These reactions to her must be a fluke caused by…something. Perhaps a contaminate in Earth's atmosphere.

Weak.

"Hi, Kai." Nixy smiled at him, her lips as red as her dress, and his mouth turned dry as the desert.

"Hello, Nixy." He ran his tongue over his lips and inclined his head. "I appreciate you allowing me to use the roof to come and go this evening."

Breathe and focus.

That was the only way to recapture some semblance of sanity over his body's inappropriate responses.

"You're welcome. Are you ready?" She gestured toward the street with one hand. "The restaurant is just a couple of blocks away. Walking distance."

"Aye, I am." He stepped smoothly to her side.

"Let's go then."

Nixy gazed over the top of her menu at Kai. "So, what do you think?"

He pursed his lips in an adorable way, his full attention had been riveted on her as she'd read the menu to him. "I believe I will have the prawn vindaloo."

"Wow."

"Do you think that is bad?" He seemed anxious.

"Not if you were serious about loving spicy food."

His anxiety melted into a warm smile. "I am. Besides, you have already read the menu to me once. I do not wish to inconvenience you again."

"Oh, bosh." She set her menu aside. "I don't mind at all. Sorry your visual language translator is on the blink. Has that happened before?"

"Only once, when I first arrived. I will have Fyad look at it when I get back to the hotel." He patted his hand on the backless bench under him. "Thank you for making sure I was accommodated with a comfortable perch."

She grinned at him. "No problem."

It wasn't the first time she'd taken an off-worlder out to

explore Earth. Although, this was the first time she'd been attracted to her guest. And wasn't that an interesting turn of events?

The waiter picked that moment to pop in and take their order, then he collected their menus and hurried away.

"So." She took a sip of ice water, swallowing it down before continuing. "You must miss home."

He nodded. "I do."

She held his gaze waiting for him to go on, but he didn't. Okay, then. It was on her to kick start this conversation. "What's it like on Bezchi, especially where you live? Anything like SoCal?"

"Not like this town, but where the spaceport is, it is similar."

"You mean the desert?"

"Aye." He picked up a papadum appetizer she'd ordered for them and spread a little of the chutney on it.

She made a rolling motion with her hand. "And…?"

"And what?" He seemed surprised by her interest.

"What's it like? Hot all the time? High desert, or low? Are there seasons? What kind of plants grow there?"

Mirth danced in his eyes as he bit into the crispy food, chewed, then swallowed. "Firewings do not usually talk during a meal."

"Well, you're on Earth, my friend, and you're with me." She patted her palm against her chest. "So we're going to talk."

He was probably pulling her chain about that anyway.

Kai chuckled. "Yes, my clan and colony live in the desert regions of Bezchi. We thrive in the heat. One of my favorite

78

plants is the ember-berry bush, which produces the most delectable and spicy berries in the summer. We eat them right off the bushes as snacks."

"Wow, that's neat. I used to do that with the raspberry plants in my mom's garden when I was a kid." And still would be in her own garden if she'd inherited half her mother's green thumb. "I thought about living out in the direction of the spaceport, but the commute is longer."

"It is a fair distance, even when flying."

"When I found my cottage on this side of the mountains, I decided the desert just wasn't meant to be. Maybe after I retire, I'll move there." She leaned forward. "What's the difference between a clan and a colony?"

"A clan encompasses all phoenixes, wherever they live. A colony is a smaller enclave." His gaze drifted to her cleavage, then snapped away to study the flat-bread in his hand instead.

"I see. And do you have a monarch too, like the other clans?"

Kai raised his gaze to meet hers, but didn't say anything. Had she overstepped herself? It had seemed like an innocuous question, but the shuttered look in his eyes suggested otherwise.

"I'm sorry, Kai. You don't have to answer that."

"We do not have a monarch." He murmured the words as though they were for her ears only. A secret he shared with her, and no one else. "We have a leader we call Most Esteemed Elder. That person is always the oldest member of the clan."

"Wow. Your most esteemed elder must be ancient, then…and oh my God, I can't believe I just said that." A wave of hot embarrassment rushed to her face. "I'm sorry."

He really wasn't *that* old. Boy, she was having to apologize left and right tonight.

Kai's lips twitched, then he tipped his head back and laughed in a way that made her heart want to laugh along.

After a moment, his laughter tapered off, but his grin didn't fade. "Yes, there are several phoenixes who are older than me. And I am all right with that."

"That's probably smart. Politics sucks." She ran her finger around the rim of her water glass. "My dad was in local and state politics, and I hated being the child-prop of his 'picture perfect family.'"

Kai frowned. "It is difficult being the fledgling of a public leader. As a rule, our monarchs keep their heirs separated from their duties."

"Heh. I can certainly appreciate that." Nothing like a scandal to convince anyone to stay as far from the lime-light as possible. "That's why I became a nice, quiet, boring accountant. You said you didn't have parents, so who took care of you?"

"The simple answer is the female who was the most esteemed elder when I arrived."

Her mouth popped open. "Your *leader* does that?"

"It is the traditional duty of the most esteemed when a new infant arrives." His grin was borderline charming. "You could say that Fya was my mother figure, though many others were instrumental in my education. She left us all too soon."

"I'm sorry for your loss. I still miss my mother, and she's been gone thirty years."

"I am sorry, Nixy." He pressed his lips into a flat line and furrows appeared across his brow. "Fya left the colony to be with her soul mate. It was a time of joy for her and I do not begrudge her now. When she passed to the Great Aerie, she was very happy."

He appeared startled at his own words, as though he hadn't meant to be so candid with her.

She reached across the table and patted his arm. "I'm glad for her. And, I'm glad you had her in your life for the time you did."

The waiter returned with their food. She spent the rest of dinner in utter amazement at Kai's ability to practically inhale his super-spicy meal without breaking a sweat. Indian food was one of her favorites, but even she had to dab her upper lip and wipe away her tears a lot.

It was full dark when they made their way back to the Silverstar building. They came to a stop next to her car and she smiled up at him. "Still can't believe you wolfed all that down without any problem. I can't even imagine how hot food is from your home."

"I may have to take a sample of curry back with me. It is the most amazing spice, and should be added to everything," he announced.

She blinked, then a laugh burst out. "Well, okay then."

"You do not agree?"

"It's good and all, but I'm not sure about curry in cheesecake." Which sounded seriously gross.

"Maybe we should try it."

"Maybe." Or not.

An awkward quiet settled over them. The moment of

transition that always happened, when it was time to go, but no one wanted to be the first to say so.

She cleared her throat. "Um, what does soul mate mean?"

He blinked a couple of times, appearing to be considering his words. "I believe the best way to define it is the finding the other half of our souls."

"You never did, though? Find your soul mate, I mean."

He shook his head.

"I'm sorry, Kai." Her hand twitched, and she gave in to the desire to reach out to him.

He met her halfway, wrapping his warm fingers around hers. The touch was natural, comforting, and set her girly bits to aching.

"My life has been good, and I have no regrets." His smile was slow, but genuine. "And tonight has been one of my favorite life experiences."

A pleasant warmth rose to her cheeks. "Mine too."

"Good night, Nixy." He raised her hand and pressed his lips to its back.

"'Night, Kai."

He released his hold on her and strode toward the building. Without her. No invitation to fly her to his hotel room for a nightcap, or anything. Not that that was what she wanted, but she'd be lying to herself if she said she hadn't expected something. Was dating etiquette that much different on his world?

Kai paused at the door like something had occurred to him, and hope glimmered in her heart.

He turned to face her. "Nixy?"

"Yes, Kai?"

"I hope we can do this again."

A smile tugged at the corners of her mouth. "Me too."

And with that, he stepped through the doorway and the door closed, blocking her view of him. That was it, then. She blew out a long gust of air, let herself into her car, then drove home.

NINE

———————————✦———————————

The quiet of the cottage held an edge of disappointment to it as Nixy dropped her purse on the recliner in her bedroom and slipped off her shoes. The touch of Kai's lips against the back of her hand was like a promise branded to her skin. Except, it shouldn't feel that way. There was no future for them. Being widowed a second time held about as much appeal as repeatedly slamming her hand in a car door. And the age gap between them made being left alone again a frightening reality.

No, it wasn't reasonable to have anything more than a friendship with him.

Says the woman who is so weirdly attracted to him.

She unzipped her dress, slid it down her legs, and draped it on the chair with her purse. It must be those crazy dreams that made the lines between fantasy and reality blur. Although, after tonight, the older "real" version of Kai had become quite a bit more appealing. And that shirt he wore, dayum. Normally his eyes looked black, but tonight there had been a definite purple hue to them.

Argh, no. Keep things professional.

He'd eventually go back to Bezchi, and then where'd she be? She glanced at the photo on her nightstand.

"It'll be just you and me again, babe."

She headed into the bathroom and cranked the faucet to fill the tub, then tugged her girdle and undergarments off, leaving them on the tile floor. They'd be fine there until tomorrow. She climbed into the tub and sank down to recline in the steamy water.

Despite the awkward end to their evening, it *had* been a wonderful dinner. They'd talked about so much, and Kai had even given her a peek into his childhood. How sad he had never found his soul mate, though. A piece of their conversation surfaced, and she sat up so fast water sloshed over the side.

"He said *phoenix*." But that couldn't possibly mean the same thing as the creature from Earth mythology, could it?

No, that was ridiculous. Kyzel and Rol both resembled hawks or eagles, but that didn't mean they hovered on air currents hunting rodents for dinner. And Fyad had a definite crowish look going, and she'd never seen him hopping around fresh road-kill or collecting sparkly things, that was for sure.

She relaxed back into the water. Phoenix must just a term for…people who lived in the desert and liked to eat spicy food. Fiery food. Yes, that was it, end of discussion. She wasn't going to think about it anymore. In fact, after her bath, she was going to read until her eyes couldn't stay open. Then she was going to fall into a nice deep sleep.

And she absolutely, positively *would not* dream.

Something about the dream had changed. The pond water was cool around Nixy's ankles, and the sun was warm on her shoulders. Even the stones lining the bank were hard and cold under her butt. How come she'd never noticed the little sensory details before?

Because this time I'm only wearing my nightie.

She ran her hands over the smooth, silky black fabric of her favorite negligée. One she'd bought after Efrem's death because she couldn't bring herself to wear any of the ones he'd made love to her in. Some of the other widows in her support group had looked at her funny when she'd admitted that, but one thing she'd learned was that everyone grieved differently.

Anyway, the winery was beautiful this time. And since this was a dream, she could wear whatever she damn well pleased because no one was here to judge her.

A choked gasp came from behind, and she twisted partway around. "*Kai.*"

Of course he'd be here, in his usual younger dream form. But what wasn't usual was his outfit. No shirt or Bezchian flying leathers covered the golden skin of his bare chest, as they did in real life. Just loose white pants riding lower on his hips than she'd ever seen....

Me-ow, Kai.

"Ni-Nixy?" His gaze traveled down to her breasts, and back up. "You look as lovely now as you did at dinner."

Oh, dear. Her boobs were spilling out of the negligée, and all her body rolls weren't being contained by her girdle. A burning heat raced to her cheeks and she turned back around to face the pond, crisscrossing her arms over her breasts. Not everyone looked as hot as him in their sleep clothes.

"No." Kai stepped closer and kneeled at her side. "You are beautiful. I mean it."

A small huff escaped her. "This is a dream, so you're saying what I want you to say. Even I know that."

Surprise flashed in his eyes, which up close like this were still the darkest purple imaginable. "What if I am saying what *I* want to say?"

"Well, you can't be. It's my dream, right?" And she'd prove it to him. She forced her arms to move, reaching up to slide her hands behind his neck, and draw him to her.

It was supposed to have been a slow, lazy kind of kiss. Instead, the moment she touched her mouth to his, a fire of need exploded inside, racing through her with wild abandon, and suddenly it was all tongues in a desperate dance of desire. She pressed against him, and he drew her onto his lap. There was no mistaking the hard length under her butt cheek for anything other than his erection. God help her.

Kai cupped his hand over her breast, tweaking her nipple. A shot of white-hot lust arced straight down between her legs. If there was any question about his intent before, it was gone now.

"God, Kai." *Don't stop.*

He pulled back with a growl, then kissed his way over her jaw and down her neck to her breast. All she had to do was arch just a little and…. The heat of his mouth closing over the hard bud drew a groan from deep inside her. And the way

87

he sucked on it through the thin material had her rocking her hips against his thigh.

A flash of panic spiked in her gut. What was she doing? Things had gone too far, even for a dream. She wasn't ready for this yet.

I need space...and air...and time to think.

She clasped her hands to either side of his head and force him to break the suction. Confusion clouded his gorgeous eyes.

"I'm sorry." It was all she could manage to choke out, then she pushed him away.

A tumbling sensation sent her spinning into blackness.

Kai awoke with a hard jerk, as if he had been dream falling out of the sky. Only the soft touch of the mattress under his belly and the faint scent of cleaning soaps from the pillow under his cheek assured him he was not laying broken on the ground. Still, tremors wracked through him and he could not seem to get enough oxygen, no matter how hard he breathed.

"It was a dream. Only a dream."

But his dream-self had *physically responded* to Nixy, desired her, and that was completely unexpected. Inappropriate. How could that happen if he was in the hotel penthouse, and she was nowhere near by?

I need to meditate; clear my mind.

He forced his eyes open and shifted his hips to alleviate the pressure of the hard thing pressing against his lower abdomen. Whatever was under him moved too, tugging at his groin. That was not a sensation he had ever experienced before. Had something creeped into his bed as he had slept?

He braced his hands against the mattress, levered his body up, and gazed down. There was nothing on the sheet. But his cock was fully extended, standing straight up, pointing accusingly at him. The evenly spaced fleshy bands of his pleasure rings fluctuated. None of these things had ever happened before. Not to him.

"No." He drew his legs under him and sat back on his heels. Then he prodded at his erection with his finger, pushing it downward toward its normal position.

It bounced back up, bobbing as though laughing at him.

Panic knotted in his gut and his breathing became erratic. This was wrong, all wrong. A phoenix only responded like this in the *presence* of their soul mate. But Nixy was not here, so this must be residual from the dream. And she was not his soul mate anyway, so how had this happened?

He had to do something about his…*condition*…before his daily report to Uri, but what? He let his gaze dart around the room until the bathroom door caught his attention. A shower. Aye, a nice hot shower would relax him.

He crawled across the bed, stretching his wings out far enough to keep his balance. The second his bare feet connected with the short-pile carpeting, he stumbled toward the bathroom.

Wham. Crash.

"*Ow*." He retracted his wings and glanced at the bedside lamp now teetering on its rounded side, shade askew. "Sorry. I will fix you later."

After he had fixed his *other* problem.

He shimmied through the bathroom door sideways, so as not to bang his wings into the immovable door frame, then pulled the shower lever to the on position. The water flowed from the flat, silver device at the far end of the all-but-useless circular fixture called a *bathtub*.

Even after all the days he had been here, he had yet to figure out how to fit into the thing comfortably. The best he had managed was to dip one wing in at a time to clean them, then draw them in against his back as tight as possible and soak his body on his hands and knees. In this case, humans were fortunate to not have wings.

Perhaps he and Fyad should return to the Silverstar suite, where everything was sized appropriately for a Bezchian. Even Prime Advisor Rol's displeasure dimmed at the prospect of taking a real bath again.

Steam flowed around him as he stepped under the miniature artificial rain shower, then gazed down at his still stiff-appendage.

Why is it not going down?

Maybe it needed help. He gave it a push with his finger, again. No, that did not work any better than it had the first time. More force must be required. He wrapped his hand around it and…. Jolts of pleasure had him sucking in a deep breath. Oh, sweet spring breezes, he had heard that cocks could be sensitive when aroused, but like this?

And if he moved his hand just so…. The ridge rings pulsated against his palm like living things, and his abdominal muscles tightened. He closed his eyes and a groan escaped him. What sheer bliss was this?

Nixy.

He opened his eyes and jerked his hand away as though it had been burned. It could not be her. She was not present.

Then explain this.

An anomaly, nothing more. One he could get control over, somehow. He glanced up at the rain disc. If hot water did not fix it, maybe cold water would. He cranked the lever to the other side and the water went from pleasantly hot to steal-his-breath freezing.

A roar of misery lodged in his throat even as his body contracted in a hard shudder. Stinging icy torment, that is what this was. He looked down and almost laughed with relief. Torture or not, his cock was relaxing, softening to its normal position. Clearly his body's reaction had been caused by a dream only, not Nixy herself. What a relief that there was no chance this would ever happen when she was near him.

A prick of disappointment pinched at his heart, but he tamped it down and shut off the water. Such feelings served no purpose. He gave his wings a shake, expelling a fine spray of excess water onto the bathing room's walls, then reached for a towel and wiped the nubby material over his body.

Now that he was back in control, he must prepare for his communications with Uri. He dressed quickly, then settled on the desk perch in front of the deep-space communicator. A moment later, it pinged a signal from the most esteemed.

"Greetings, Elder Kai." Uri's voice crackled over the tiny speaker, but no visual appeared this time.

It was not unusual to have audio-only on such communiques, even though he had expected a visual call. "Greetings, Most Esteemed."

"What is your report?"

"The plan to befriend Ms. Vogel is moving forward. She responded positively to the *bouquet*, and we consumed a meal together at a public place. Also...."

Uncertainty gripped him. Sharing details of the evening seemed somehow wrong. Too personal.

"Also, what?" Uri prompted.

He ran his tongue over his suddenly dry lips. "I believe she is responding much better than we hoped. She has allowed me to infiltrate her dreams."

The silence from Uri was worrisome, and as it lengthened, Kai shifted on the perch. The communicator box glowed a pale blue, indicating the connection was good, so why was Uri not speaking?

"Most Esteemed?"

"I am here." Uri's voice was monotone.

"Is there a problem?"

"I am not certain." Uri sounded unsettled. "Proceed as you are, but, Kai...."

"Aye?"

"She is human and may think your overtures are more than platonic, so be careful."

"Aye, thank you, Most Esteemed."

The blue glow faded as the connection ended, and he hunched his shoulders. In his concern over telling Uri too much, why had it not occurred to him that his revered leader might be keeping something from him as well?

TEN

Frustration was like a living thing writhing just under Nixy's skin. Not even kicking along the sidewalk through wet orange, yellow, and brown leaves in the pouring rain was helping. Perfect Sunday afternoon walking weather for someone from Seattle, maybe, but not so much for a SoCal girl.

Still, it was a relief to escape the stifling confines of her tiny cottage. Kai had called twice today, already, and both times she'd let it go to voicemail. How could she face him, talk to him, knowing she'd come so close to having dream sex with him? What if something she said gave it away and he guessed? Wouldn't that be humiliating?

As humiliating as losing my job?

God, she didn't even want to think about that. It was easier to pretend Jordan wouldn't be in her office in about forty-eight hours to fire her. And what would happen to Adam once she was gone? Maybe Jordan would promote him to fill the vacancy, which would be great. For Adam.

She swallowed against the lump in her throat. All her high

93

hopes for her future were on a collision course with the side of Mt. Jacinto.

More like Mt. Everest.

Becoming an agent for the Silverstar Agency had been a daring step out of the nondescript, vanilla comfort zone she'd built for herself. Dad's affair with the wife of his political rival had pushed her and Mom into the center ring of a circus she'd never wanted to attend. Since then, she'd lived her life trying not to be noticed.

Until Efrem. Too bad he'd never know how much his calm and steady confidence in her had given her the courage to apply for a job she loved. A job that'd given her so much joy.

"Thanks, babe." The steady drum of rain against her yellow rain slicker muffled her murmured words, but that was okay. They were only for her and Efrem anyway.

She slapped through the puddles that had formed in the low spots on the sidewalk as a resigned sense of inevitability settled over her. It seemed only fair that she give Adam a head's up about what she'd done.

A low grumble of thunder rumbled in the distance—her cue to head home, even though she still hadn't figured out what to do about Kai or the feelings he had raised in her. Feelings that had somehow managed to cross over between her dreams and real life.

She tugged the hood of her rain slicker forward as she turned onto her street. A couple of minutes later, she trudged up her front walk and let herself inside. Warm air floated over her like a hug from an old friend. She peeled off her layers, and laid out her raingear to dry.

Now what? There were plenty of little piddly projects to work on, but everything seemed so…uninspiring.

She moved aimlessly into the kitchen and drew back the curtain to stare through the gray evening light at the covered patio. Rain dripped down the brick chimney of the built-in barbeque and puddled at its base.

Between dream-Kai, real Kai, and her looming meeting with Jordan, it was a wonder she didn't have a migraine. Well, there was always tomorrow for that, especially since she was not going to sleep tonight. What did she have to lose anyway? Besides the first job she'd ever loved, of course. And the old guy from another planet who she wanted to bang in the worst way, even though he didn't seem interested in her. Not in *that* way, at least.

Screw it. She dropped the curtain back into place. Time for dinner.

A bowl and a half of lentil soup and a slice of sourdough bread later, she snuggled down on the couch with a book. A medical thriller, because the goal was to stay awake all night. By the second chapter, her eyelids drooped.

I should make some coffee….

"Something has you worried."

That was Kai's voice, from right behind her. Her heartrate went from slow trot to giddy up. He stepped up next to her and lowered himself to sit at her side on the pond's stone embankment.

Dammit. I fell asleep anyway.

The walk in the rain, soup, and reading on the couch had conspired against her. Relaxed her too much. She should've taken a hot bath and crawled into bed for all the good fighting sleep had done. At least she was wearing sensible Bermuda shorts and a T-shirt this time.

She lowered her gaze to the surface of the pond, to her bare toes visible under the tepid water. "I may lose my job on Tuesday."

He turned his head sharply toward her. "Why?"

"I did something stupid." A little humorless laugh slipped out. "Actually, it comes down to not being as careful as I should've been. About seven months ago, Silverstar updated their application process. As usual, I did a faux dry run of the process to make sure I understood it, because, you know, I'm not the most computer-savvy person in the world. If any of my clients had questions, I wanted to be able to help them.

"Anyway, I really shouldn't have worried; the whole thing is incredibly user friendly. But, when I went to delete it, I somehow submitted it instead."

"I do not understand." He frowned. "Your actions were driven by responsibility. What is the problem?"

"I filled it out with all of my personal info, and downloaded and tested the bio-scan app. And that's against company policy. I have no idea why it's taken so long for my supervisor to figure it out, other than I used my full name, not my nickname. That might have thrown her off because everyone calls me Nixy." She covered her face with her hands. "I don't know what went wrong, but I've been trying to fix it ever since."

"What is your full name?"

Of everything she'd said, *that* was what he focused on? She allowed her hands to slide down to her lap. "A stupid name my wanna-be-trendy parents picked out that always got me teased in school. Never mind."

She caught the motion of his nod in her peripheral vision, and silence settled between them like an unspoken agreement. Nothing but the two of them, the breeze in the willow tree, and the burbling fountain in the opposite end of the pond.

And that damn burning sensation under her skin, yearning for more. It was like she couldn't escape it, even in her sleep.

So, why not go with it?

She frowned and drew her brows together. Would it work? If she had dream sex with Kai, would it make the need go away?

Kai's soft cough cut through her musings. "Nixy…your clothing…."

She looked down. Holy moly! Her shorts and T-shirt had turned into her red negligée this time. She shifted her gaze to Kai's pants, now the same ones as last time—because apparently she'd liked them that much. And, oh my, that was one obvious tent under the crotch fabric.

She swallowed hard against the nervous anticipation in her throat. Well, this was her dream after all, and she could do anything she damn well pleased.

And the idea of doing Kai sounded delicious. She drew her feet out of the water and turned to meet his gaze. Desire that matched hers glowed in his gorgeous eyes.

That'd be an all systems, go for her.

She launched herself at him and he caught her, his red-feathered wings flaring out before he landed on his back on the grass.

Then she was on him, in him, exploring his mouth with her tongue. God help her, he even tasted of cinnamon.

Of course he does, because that's what I want.

"Nixy."

Dayum, the way he moaned her name against her mouth was sexy. His hand over her breast was sexy. His fingers tweaking her hard nipples was sexy. The friction of his rod against her girly bits through two layers of clothing was sexy.

"Kai, you're the sexiest fucking man alive. And you smell so good."

Kai surged up, rolling them so she was under him. "I want you. In your dreams, in reality…I. Want. You. Nixy Vogel."

"Then take me. Because I don't think I can stand not having you in me for much longer."

The man didn't need to be told twice. He rose up enough to help her bunch up her negligée to her hips and tug his pants down. Then he speared into her, hard and hot.

His groan of extasy matched hers, long and low, then he muttered words she didn't catch. And even that was sexy.

He touched his forehead to hers. "I never expected… never knew…."

"Move Kai, now. In and out." She nudged him with her hips, and he moved. Awkwardly at first, then with more confidence. "Oh. My. *God.*"

She bucked up to meet his thrusts, panting as a fluttering sensation stroked the walls of her channel with exquisite pleasure. "Oh…Jesus…what…?" Her entire body was electric, riding the cusp of the fastest orgasm she'd ever had. "Harder, Kai. I won't break."

And bless him, he did, rocking her world with a grunt accompanying each plunge.

"Nixy…I…." His face scrunched as if he was trying to hold back.

"Come with me, Kai. Let it go. *Hard.*"

He slammed into her once, twice, and a wave of pleasure shattered over her. "*Yes!*"

Kai shouted as she clamped down around him, buried inside her to his base as she pushed up to meet him, milk him for everything he gave. He shuddered, then sighed as his body relaxed over her.

She drifted in a haze of well-being, cradling Kai in her arms and between her legs. One thing was for sure: dream sex just might be better than real sex.

ELEVEN

———◆———

Kai lay still in his bed, wings stretched out on the Bezchian-sized mattress, head turned to one side. Exactly the same position he had been in when he had woken up from Nixy's dream. If he did not move, then perhaps time would not either.

But, the dark of night had given way to the morning light now glowing around the edges of the black-out shades of the Silverstar traveler's nest. And the numbers on the nightstand clock moved forward another minute.

About the only good thing about being back in the suite was that Prime Advisor Rol seemed to have disappeared. Ah, the freedom of having no one to distract him from his ever-present crippling sense of doom.

A long, low groan rose up from the deepest trenches of his being. They had had *sex*. In the dreamwalk. But phoenixes could not copulate with anyone but their soul mate. So, what did it mean?

She is my soul mate.

But, it was a dreamwalk, and she is human, so that was not possible.

Am I sure about that?

He was not.

Yet, the evidence of his body's response was stuck to the sheet under his belly. There was no denying that what happened in the dreamwalk had been mimicked in reality. So, again, what did it mean?

It means I failed my clan again.

That knowledge did not seem as mortifying as it had before. But Uri would want to know, so what would be the best way to present it to him? *Greetings, Most Esteemed. I had sex with a human in a dreamwalk, and enjoyed it. I want to do it with her again, but in reality next time. By the by, has this ever happened to a phoenix before?*

The answer of course would be no, followed by a lengthy monologue about the duties of a mate-matcher. At this point, the only thing that might save him was to prove Silverstar was a sham…which was something he no longer believed.

He squeezed his eyes shut, then blinked a couple of times. Besides, there was no way he could hurt Nixy.

Ah, and Nixy…. The memory of her soft body moving under him, the taste of her full, coral-tipped breasts on his tongue, the way her female parts had clamped down on him as he had exploded inside her. It had been glorious, exquisite, intimate. Life-defining.

She would be preparing for her work day by now. This, possibly her last full day at a job she was passionate about. It would crush her to be terminated, and that was something he could relate to, having been denied the privilege of mate-matching for at least as long as she had been alive.

Wait. If that was right, his matching problem started around the time Nixy was born. Coincidence?

The clock numbers advanced again. Now he understood what an Earth minute was. It was all at once a short increment of time, and it was an eternity. More so when it seemed like he would have to choose between his heritage or Nixy.

He turned his face into the soft pillow and let out a howl. The release of his inner turmoil in this manner brought his thoughts into sharper focus.

What he needed was a plan. First, seek counsel from the most esteemed elder. No, wait. First get out of bed and clean up, *then* see if he could reach Uri on the deep space communicator. And this time he wanted to see the most esteemed's face. After that, make a plan based on that discussion. Not a perfect strategy but it was a start.

He levered himself up with his arms and stared at the wet mark on the sheets. If the situation had not been real enough before, it certainly was now. Something was happening between him and Nixy, and the only one who might confirm it was Uri.

A gentle feminine chuckle came from his left and he snapped his head up. Fya stood at the side of the bed, a bemused expression on her face.

This was an unexpected development. He sat back on his heels. "Another timeslip, Most Esteemed?"

"Aye, youngling—the last one, I promise. And I am not your most esteemed elder any longer." Her gaze flicked to the sheets, then back to him. "It seems you are at a crucial point in your life, Kai."

He lowered his gaze to the wet spot. "It is difficult to comprehend what any of this means."

"I know. And I cannot make the choice for you."

"Can you advise me?" He gave her a pleading look.

"If you ask the right questions."

This would be more difficult than he had hoped, but there were so many unanswered questions that had haunted him for too long. "Why have I failed in my duties?"

"You have not failed. Your calling is higher than just the mere duties of a phoenix mate-matcher."

"I suppose coming to Earth is part of that?"

"Aye, it is."

All right, that helped, a bit. "Strange things have been happening since I came here. I have formed an attachment to a human female—a forbidden attachment."

Fya sat on the bed, but the mattress did not dip under her weight. "What do you remember overhearing in the meditation garden the day you listened in on my private conversation with Uri?"

All of it, much to his continued shame. "You said you knew Avok was your soul mate because of the way your body responded to him, and because you dreamwalked with him."

She lowered her chin and gave him a knowing look. "Sound familiar?"

"Aye." He choked out the word. "But with a human...?"

"Last time we spoke, I told you that change was coming, and you would be at the center."

"But, this is...scandalous." And had he not caused enough of that in this incarnation?

"No, Kai, this is *change*, and there is no reason to fear it, for you are Bezchi. Tell me, what did you feel when you were in the presence of the new monarchs of the Raptorclaw clan?

He drew his brows together. "I sensed respect, honor, and passion. A level of commitment I have never sensed in the matches I have made. And intimacy."

"Love is indeed rare." Fya's smile turned wistful. "It is a spark that makes a match truly special."

"But we do not match for love, why?"

"You will ask Uri that question. It is time he come up with an answer to that one." She patted his hand. "Now, I have one more question for you: what do you feel when you look at Phoenix Vogel?"

Phoenix who? Wait, did she mean, *Nixy*? Phoenix was Nixy's given name? And the emotional mess that had bubbled inside him since he had met her was…. "That is love?"

A gentle emotion shimmered in Fya's eyes. "What do *you* think, youngling?"

Confusion, joy, fear, awe; it all flooded into his heart, filling it to near bursting. He placed one hand over it and lowered his gaze. His cock was hardening, and it was because of Nixy. Just the thought of her now did this to him.

"Soul mate." He murmured the word, but it was not enough. "*Soul mate!*"

His shout echoed in the empty room. Fya was gone, but she had guided him well. Nixy was his everything, he could see that now. Could accept the wonderous gift of her, of love.

Nixy strode off the elevator like a woman on a mission. Not a *saving all humanity/fireworks and glory* kind of mission; more like a self-preservation mission. A mission to keep her dreams to herself.

Especially last night's dream. Just thinking about it was as bad as having a hot flash. Good God, give her an air-conditioner cranked to full arctic blast mode.

Mom always said I had a vivid imagination.

Adam looked up from whatever he was doing on his computer. "Happy Monday, boss. You're in early."

"If Elder Kai shows up, do *not* let him in." *I can't face him now.*

She stepped into her office and the door slid shut behind her. Alone, finally. And she'd made it without getting grilled by Adam.

Swoosh.

"You can't just *do* that." Adam swept into the room.

Crap. So much for a clean escape. "Do what?"

She shrugged off her jacket, slid it onto a hanger then hung it in the tiny closet.

Oh, look. The fire extinguisher.

Ack. Was *everything* going to remind her of him?

Adam placed his hands on her desk and leaned forward. "I've known you long enough to figure out when something's going on."

Yeah, something was going on all right. Heat rose in her cheeks.

Adam inhaled an exaggerated gasp. "You didn't have *sex* with him, *did you*?"

The heat flamed to something just a degree or two shy of a fireball.

"Oh. My. God." He did the I'm-stunned-beyond-belief, slow sink into one of the client chairs. "It's just you and me here, and we're not on the clock for another fifteen minutes. Besides," he shrugged. "I have something to talk to you about too. But you go first."

"What's going on?"

"Ah, ah, ah." He shook his head like a disapproving parent.

"Fine." She raised her hands in an *I give up* gesture and plopped her butt into her own chair. "There's not much to tell. We had a nice dinner, he walked me back to my car, and kissed my hand like a gentleman. Then I went home and had very intense and explicit dreams about him."

"Ooh." Adam waggled his eyebrows. "No wonder you don't want to see him."

Oh, she wanted to see him all right. Clothes on. Clothes off. In nothing but his flying leathers.

Can I get one of those in my size?

Nope. No way. None of that was going to happen.

She cleared her throat and folded her hands on the desk in front of her. "Your turn. What's up?"

His smile dimmed a fraction. "Well, I have good news and bad news—"

"Stop." She raised one hand. "Most important thing: Are you leaving me?"

"No."

"Good."

"Not yet." He did a full-face grimace as if bracing for her to go nuclear.

Dammit. "A-*dam.*"

"Okay, okay. Here's the deal." He shifted in the chair and licked his lips. "My thirty-fifth birthday is coming up this year, and it hit me a few months ago that I'm not getting any younger and maybe I should think about settling down. So, I submitted an application to the NebulaX Agency."

"The intergalactic LGBTQ matching agency?" Not a direct competitor, per se. "That's really smart."

"Not really." Adam's shoulders sagged as though he'd deflated. "I think that's why Ms. Jones is coming to talk to you."

"What? Because of *you?*"

"It's one thing to apply to NebX, and another now that they've found half my triad match."

Well, yeah, that could be a problem. "Triad mate unions aren't recognized on Earth."

"Not *yet.* And I have a little time, at least." He grinned. "Korob, my male mate, is due to arrive on Earth next month."

"That's *wonderful.*"

"That part is. But the part that Ms. Jones might have found out, not so much." He sighed. "I suppose getting fired would leave me with plenty of free time to get to know him while we wait for our female partner match. But being unemployed isn't the most ideal way to begin a relationship."

Definitely not. "You know I'll always have your back."

Even if she wasn't still around. She leaned back in her chair. "But I don't think you're going to have to worry. I'm pretty sure you and your triad are not the reason Jordan is visiting."

Adam frowned. "Why? What's going on?"

Time for some truth. "I accidently submitted a false application with all my personal info on it."

"To Silverstar?" She gave him a nod and his eyes went as round as she'd ever seen them. "What the hell, Nixy? How did *that* happen?"

She explained the situation as succinctly as she could, then shrugged. "So, now do you see my point?"

"Yeah." He rubbed the blond scruff on his chin. "Want me to take a look at it?"

"If you were a techie, I would've asked you months ago." There was no one else she'd trust to handle this more than Adam, if he had the IT skills. "Besides, if Jordan knows, it's already too late."

"Right, there is that." Adam sighed. "Well, if you think of anything, I've got your back too, you know."

"I know." Most reliable guy in the universe.

TWELVE

Kai slid off the bed and ran out of his room toward the common room. He certainly had questions for Most Esteemed Elder Uri now, and seeing his expression as he answered was vital.

"*Eek*." Raven Crawford's shriek stopped him in the doorway. "You're *naked*."

Oh, blessed eternal ones, when had Fyad's mate arrived? Humans were a prudish lot, unlike phoenixes. Nudity was never a concern at home because none of them were ever interested in each other sexually. As for the other four clans, they had always accepted the occasional slip-up from his kind.

Fyad stepped between them, wings partially extended and a glower on his face. "Elder Kai, please cover yourself."

"Aye, of course." He snatched a cushion off one of the table perches and held it in front of his semi-stiff appendage. "My apologies. I will be in the communication room."

He hurried in the direction of the room before either of them acknowledged his statement, or demanded he return to his room and properly dress before coming out again. There was no time for fragile sensibilities at this moment.

He sent a hail to Uri, then sat back to wait.

The image of Uri's face came into focus, hovering over the softly glowing device. "Greetings, Elder Kai. You may proceed with today's update."

"Greetings, Most Esteemed Elder, and thank you. I will make this quick."

Concern rose in Uri's eyes. "Is all well?"

"Why do we not match mates for love?" The words tumbled from him, and he leaned against the edge of the table as if to better hear his leader's response.

Uri's mouth fell opened, his surprise evident. "Why do you ask?"

"I just had a conversation with Fya in a timeslip of her creation. She told me to ask you."

Uri shook his head, and his wings drooped. "She did warn me."

"She *did*? When?"

"The day she left the colony." The eldest elder shrugged his shoulders. "You will eventually learn about this, but may not discuss it with any phoenix younger than six hundred sun migrations. Do you understand?"

"That will not be a problem." If all went as he hoped, he would not be returning to the colony anyway.

"Very well, then," Uri said. "Many thousands of sun migrations ago, long before my time even, we did arrange love matches between the clans."

"You mean *within* the clans."

"No, I mean *between*. The four clans of the monarchies

were not limited to mates within their own clans. Too often, such matches led to disputes, and one led to an all-out war that nearly wiped out all of us. We feared for the future of all, including ourselves who can only mate with non-phoenixes.

"So, we proposed a solution. Cross-matching between the clans would no longer happen. The clans would be matched with members of their own only. Since phoenixes are long-lived, it would allow us to track the matings within the clans to avoid inbreeding and keep them strong. The occasional infusion of phoenix DNA also helps when a phoenix finds their soul mate."

Kai stared open-mouthed at Uri's image. That was enlightening, to say the least. "But, why is it a secret? Why do the clans not know?"

And how much more history are you…we…hiding from them?

"It was part of the agreement. To bury the animosity and hate, and foster positive relations between the monarchies, was the goal. Now, thousands of sun migrations later, the system is working. The clans cooperate, work together, depend on one another. There are no ancient grievances in their memories to stop them from flourishing, and this is the way it must remain. We cannot afford to return to the past. Cannot risk losing our civilization again."

"No." He ran his tongue over his lips. He must word this properly on behalf of the clans. Failure was not an option. "I have felt the connection between two love matches since arriving on Earth. Love is strong. Love does not lead to destruction, but hate and greed do. Soul mates are love personified, and not once has our planet gone to war over a soul mate pair."

"Pah." Uri waved one hand in dismissal. "You know nothing about the soul mate bond yet, youngling."

"I do know, Most Esteemed, because my soul mate is Nixy Vogel." *Phoenix. Her name is Phoenix.* What were the odds?

Uri's wide-eyed, open-mouthed expression would be comical in almost any other situation, but not now. "That is *impossible.*"

"Then why have I shared multiple dreamwalks with her? Why does degrading her with my words make me physically ill? Why does my blood sing a song of fire in my veins whenever she is near me? And why has my body awakened to her."

"Your body?" Uri whispered. "How?"

"I do not know, but the power of what I feel for her is undeniable."

Uri sat up straighter. "You are young still, too young to find your soul mate."

"With all respect, Most Esteemed, I disagree."

"No good will come of it, Kai. It is enough that both Kyzel *and* Rol have now defied tradition. I will not allow you to be influenced by them."

The prime advisor had mated? "That is *proof* that humans are compatible with us. The addition of their DNA into our gene pool would strengthen us."

Uri furrowed his brow, as if giving the idea consideration. "It will not happen. If you take this human as a mate, you will be too old to breed. As are the Raptorclaw monarch and the prime advisor."

"But others are not, and should be free to choose their mates." Singling out Fyad and Raven right now would only bring the younglings trouble. "Phoenixes will know which unions are true, and can still bless those with the elements of love." His clan would still have a role in society.

The stubborn set of Uri's jaw did not bode well. "Return home immediately, Elder Kai."

"As soon as I have successfully completed my mission, Most Esteemed Elder." He gave his hand a wave over the communicator and Uri's image was gone in a blip.

He let his wings relax and blew out a gust of air. There would be no going home, despite Uri's order. Defying his leader, a male he deeply respected, went against everything he believed. Could this be the change Fya spoke of? The moment in which the future of his home-world rested on his wings? What right did he have to send the lives of all Bezchians in a new direction without their consent?

Yet, what would happen to them if he denied his connection to Nixy's soul? Pain stabbed at his heart leaving him gasping. He curled inward, drawing his wings around himself. Rejecting her would end him, but what would it do to Bezchi?

You are Bezchi. Fya's words whispered to him, and she had never lied to him.

"If my destiny and Bezchi's are entwined, then there is only one choice."

Nixy.

My soul mate.

It was a miracle to have found her so early in his life. An incredible blessing. A gift.

But she has no idea.

A sense of rightness and determination welled up in him, and he pressed his lips together. Just exactly how could he convince her of the truth? Open her heart during the waking time, not just in her dreams?

He exited the communication room with a renewed sense of purpose in his heart…and a pillow over his cock. His plan was merely half formed, and he had next to no idea how to execute it. If only technology was one of his fortes—

"Just *shut it*, Fyad." Raven's voice intruded on his thoughts. "If I finish this story, I'll be another step closer to getting out of that shit-hole."

Fyad snorted. "So you can be a *real* reporter?"

"*Yes.*"

Kai raised his gaze to the ceiling with a silent plea for patience from the eternal ones. How could these two be so blind to what was right in front of them? It boggled the mind.

Wait a moment. He came to a stop just outside the communication room, his gaze riveted on Fyad. The youngling guard had helped him with his computer research on Earth's other matching agencies. It had been a trial and error experience, but it would have been next to impossible without his help. It would be a simple thing to repay him for his assistance. After just one more tiny request.

"*Fyad.*"

The guard startled and turned his head. "Yes, Elder?"

"Have you learned any more about Earth computers?"

"I—"

"He doesn't know squat." Raven shot a smug look at the bodyguard. "It's me you should ask. I do a lot of investigative work and have to nose around in places where people don't want me."

That was no surprise. But she did have her portable foldable computer, which would be handy for the idea unfurling in his mind. "Ah, but you also cannot keep a secret."

"That much is true," Fyad grumbled.

Raven grinned. "I work for the Raptorclaw clan now, and *they* are my priority."

Fyad scoffed. "But, you are still employed by *Blast off!*."

"Not for long."

"Stop." Kai raised one hand, and both younglings shut their beaks. "I need help drafting a Silverstar application. Would you be kind enough to assist me, Ms. Crawford, Fyad?"

The younglings looked at each other, then at him.

"Sure."

"Of course, Elder."

"Perfect." He grinned at them. "Will you access the application for Silverstar while I go appropriately cover myself?"

"On it." Raven turned back to her compact Earth device.

He hurried back to his room, dressed with more speed than normal for his age, and returned to the common area. It took over an hour to fill out the form, mostly because Fyad and Raven could not seem to stop themselves from debating everything from the definition of a given question to the exact wording of answers.

"There we go." Ms. Crawford typed the final word with a flourish of her hands on the keyboard. "One completed application for the Silverstar Agency. Ms. Vogel isn't gonna be happy about you putting yourself out there like this, though, I can tell ya."

He frowned in her direction. "What do you mean?"

"Didn't you have a date with her the other night?"

How did she know about that?

"See?" Fyad spread his arms. "I was right. You cannot keep a secret."

Ah. That was how. It seemed Fyad could not keep a secret either.

Raven snorted. "So, should I press send, your Elderliness?"

"Is there a way to save it on a portable device that is compatible with other Earth computers, instead?"

"Sure, but you need a thumb drive." She picked up her bag and rooted through it. "I have a couple of spares in here somewhere...ah ha." She pulled out a slim, black stick-like item, inserted it into the side of the machine, then tapped some keys. "This'll just take a sec...there. Done."

She pulled the stick and handed him the tiny device. "There ya go."

"Thank you, Ms. Crawford."

"I don't know what you're waiting for, though. If I were you, I'd just get it done. The sooner you turn it in, the sooner they'll find you a match."

"He *is* a mate-matcher," Fyad grumbled. "He does not need the agency."

Here we go again.

Raven curled her upper lip. "I don't think—"

"*Stop.*" He aimed his glare from one to the other. "You

two are enough to make a mate-matcher retire to a cave. Allow me to show you something."

He reached for each of their hands, and they thankfully did not balk. Then he closed his eyes and found his center.

"What's he doing?" Raven muttered.

The soft rustle was probably Fyad's shrug, but it did not matter. As long as neither of them pulled away. He extended his senses, reaching out for their true emotions—admiration, appreciation, respect, passion—drew them in then pushed them back out, each one's to the other person.

"Oh." Raven breathed out the word like a sigh.

A wave of passion surged through the connection, the power of which he had never experienced. Using him as the conduit. This was no ordinary mate-match; it was a love match. True and pure and joyous. And he had made it, and given it his blessing as an elder. His first match in over fifty sun migrations.

He forced his eyes open, blinking away the effects of the power of mate-matching. "This is what you two have been fighting against so hard."

The younglings stared at each other, their faces alight with love.

He joined their hands together. "You are matched *love* mates for life."

The traditional words spoken when joining a pair had more meaning than ever with the addition of the word "love." The aura of the couple's feelings lingered, filling his soul with peace and satisfaction.

This was what a match should feel like.

He took two steps back. "A bond this strong should never be denied."

"Thank you, Elder." Fyad's words where full of wonder.

"Yeah." Raven breathed, then squeaked as Fyad lifted her against him.

She wrapped her legs around his middle, and they came together, locking their lips in a kiss. The raw power of the couple's passion filled the room.

"Erm." He cleared his throat. "I suggest moving into Fyad's room now."

Fyad moved forward, trapping Raven between him and the wall of the common area. For her part, Ms. Crawford delved her fingers into Fyad's black headfeathers as if she intended to meld her body to his. If either of them had heard his suggestion, they were ignoring it.

"All right, then. I will just go to my room now." No need for him, or anyone, to witness their union. "We can talk about the rest of my plan later."

Fyad undulated his hips into his mate's crotch and she moaned. Aye, time to go. Kai hurried toward the hallway, leaving the amorous couple to do their thing.

THIRTEEN

———————✦———————

Nixy leaned her head back against her desk chair and let her gaze wander around her silent office. The dimming light from the windows bathed it in the muted blue-gray tones of early evening.

I'm going to miss this place.

But, by this time tomorrow, she'd be long gone. Handed her walking papers. And there was nothing she could do to change it. Granted, there was a remote possibility that Jordan wanted to talk to her about something else entirely, but not likely.

The office door swished open and Adam leaned partway in. "Why are the lights off?"

"It's more relaxing this way."

"Ah. Got it. It's after six. You going home?"

"Soon." That was a bald-faced lie.

If she went home, she'd go to bed. And then she'd dream.

"Maybe Ms. Jones is coming for another reason."

"I thought about that. Lights on." She sat up a little straighter in her chair as the recessed lighting glowed to life in imitation day. "Guess we'll just have to wait and see what tomorrow brings."

"Yeah." He didn't look too convinced. "Want to go get a drink?"

"Nah. I'm just going to wrap things up here as much as I can before I call it a night."

Adam's half smile was equal parts sympathetic and understanding. "All right. Night, Nixy."

"Night, Adam."

The office door swished shut with a soft sigh, like her after a long but productive day.

What was she going to do with the rest of her life? Go back to accounting? Nah, that'd be a step backward. Maybe NebulaX was hiring. She had never matched LGBTQ couples...or groups like Adam's triad. That would be something new and challenging.

But, matching older couples is so rewarding.

There was something soul stirring about seeing people her age find love. Did NebX have an over-fifty department? If they didn't, maybe she could petition them and offer her services to set one up.

Her thoughts drifted to Kai. He had never found his soul mate, never experienced love the way she had. The way she could again, if she ignored that age gap and focused on what was really important: the sweet, kind, sexy pain in the butt he was.

Her channel clenched and she bit back a groan. What? Now just thinking about him made her almost come? It was a really good thing she wasn't going home tonight. There wasn't nearly enough coffee in her kitchen cabinet to keep her awake until morning.

And speaking of coffee…. She placed her palms on the desk and pushed out of her chair. May as well get the first pot started, then do a status review of all her clients to make sure everything was in order for her replacement. No one would be able to say Nixy Vogel half-assed anything. Including her own termination.

Kai leaned back against the edge of Adam's desk, wings tucked forward so as not to knock anything over, arms folded across his chest and ankles crossed. The dim night lighting gave the lobby a more intimate atmosphere. In the right situation, it could be considered romantic, if only his Nixy were here.

But she was on the other side of the wall doing who knew what, completely clueless about his presence. He opened himself to her feelings again. Her sadness, desperation, hope, and…yes, that was most definitely a flash of desire…washed through him. Was she thinking about him?

He allowed one corner of his mouth to curve up in a satisfied smirk. That was something he rarely did—smirk. But just the idea that Nixy was feeling all the same confusing things about him as he felt for her warranted such a reaction.

Just a few more minutes.

Buzz.

The sound of the cell phone vibrating on the desk next to his hip drew his attention. Raven had texted two letters, a "g" and an "o". The two younglings were ready on their end. Everything was set. Now it was up to him. The timing of his talk with Nixy—Phoenix—was crucial.

He closed his hand around the device and pushed away from the desk.

The swish of a door opening broke the silence of the lobby and Nixy stepped through the doorway. A wave of heat ripped through him with the force of a wild-fire, stronger than any of his previous reactions to her presence.

Soul mate. How had he not figured it out sooner?

Her eyes widened with a flash of surprise, and a tinge of panic. "Kai?"

"Aye." He surreptitiously flicked his thumb over the "one" button to let Raven and Fyad know contact had been made.

"What are you doing here?"

Being utterly amazed by fate. "Do you have a moment to talk?"

"Um, well." She made a fanning gesture around her face with her hands. "I have all night, I guess. Is it hot in here?"

"A bit." Hotter than a desert at high summer. He tilted his head toward her office. "Shall we?"

"Oh, uh, in my office? Sure." She seemed adorably flustered.

He followed her inside, stopping in front of her desk until she had rounded it and sat in her chair. "First, I have something for you."

He placed the phone on the desk and slid it over the glass surface, then reached into his carrying pouch and lifted out a sealed baggie of reddish-brown powder.

She frowned at it. "A bag of cinnamon?"

"Yes. It is delightfully similar to a sacred Bezchian spice we use called cinbin." *Please remember that later.*

"Okay, now I'm really confused."

"I promise it will get more confusing before it becomes clear. And for that, I am sorry."

She huffed. "Don't make me get the fire extinguisher again."

"It is probably best if you do not." The results could be disastrous. "Do you remember that I told you I was a phoenix?"

"At the restaurant. Yes." She barked a small laugh. "We have a mythology here about them, you know."

"I heard about that earlier this afternoon." Thanks to Raven. Now for the hard part. "What happens to Earth phoenixes is very similar to what happens to us."

Her eyes widened in increasing increments as his words sank in, then she slapped her hand to her mouth. "You mean, you go up in a ball of fire when you die?"

"Aye, something like that. But we call it rebirth." He gave her a crooked smile. "It happens every hundred years or so. It also happens when our soul mate confesses their love, which can be alarming to them since our soul mates are never another phoenix."

"I'm going to throw up." She did seem paler than normal.

"Nixy...*Phoenix* Vogel, please do not do that." He leaned across her desk until there was barely a hand's width between them. "We have more to discuss."

She shook her head in denial. "H…h…how did you know my name?"

"It is on the Silverstar application you accidently submitted."

"I never told you...."

"I...guessed, after sharing your dream with you last night." He would explain Fya's timeslips later.

"Oh, my God." Her cheeks turned the most brilliant and beautiful shade of red. "That was *real?*"

"Every. Last. Moment."

"Everything we did...."

"Aye. As real as my feelings for you. Hold out your hand. I have another gift for you." He waited for her to comply, then dropped the thumb drive into her hand.

"What's this?"

"If I promise to answer all your questions, will you humor me for another moment?"

"I...fine. Okay. I suppose I should plug this into the computer?"

"Please." He moved around her desk as she inserted the thumb drive. "And open the file named Future."

"It's a Silverstar application." She looked up at him, a frown marring her features. "*Your* application."

"So it is."

He reached past her, reveling in the ever-present scent of roses that surrounded her, and gave the screen a series of taps as Raven had instructed. A message popped up:

Application accepted. Please access bio-app on your communication device.

A chirp from his phone filled the silence as Nixy watched him, her lips slightly parted. He curved one wing forward, pinched a feather between his fingers, and gave it a sharp tug. The sting was no more than a sand flea bite, and as inconsequential if all went well with his plan.

He moved the feather over the phone's 5-senses reader.

Bio-app reading accepted. The Silverstar Agency thanks you for your application. You will be contacted by an agent for an interview. Your agent's name is Nixy Vogel.

"Well, that's lucky," she murmured. "You got me."

He tucked the feather into the pocket of his leggings. "I requested you on the application."

Could not afford anyone else picking it up.

"So, do I get an expla—"

Ping.

Surprise flashed in Nixy's eyes at the confirmation signal from her computer. "That was fast."

"Aye." He turned his head in unison with hers.

Match for Firewing, Kai located. Display match's bio? Y/N

Suspicion and anticipation radiated from Nixy, and he opened himself to it. To her feelings. She tapped her finger over the *Y* and another application appeared next to his, along with Nixy's photograph.

Relief and joy radiated through him. He had been right, and Silverstar had concurred. Nixy was his match and his soul mate. But, would she recognize it?

He turned her chair to face him, leaning close, and braced his hands on the armrests. "Phoenix Vogel; it is so appropriate that Phoenix is your first name."

A shaky laugh bubbled out of her, and she nodded.

He suppressed his own chuckle at the delight of watching her make the connections he had already made. "I love you,

Phoenix. You are my soul mate, my life. I burn for you in all ways, and will do so forever."

She drew in a ragged breath as tears rolled free of her eyes and over her cheeks. "This is the weirdest thing, Kai, but I lo—"

"Stop." His command was sharp enough to startle her, but she must know everything before she completed the bond. "Remember what I told you happens when a soul mate commits to a phoenix?"

"Are you about to burn up?"

"I hope so."

"God, Kai." She shook her head. "I can't do that to you."

"But, you can, my heart's flame. You must, or I cannot rejuvenate."

Tears gathered in her eyes. "I'm so scared."

"Follow Fyad's instructions when he gets here, and there will be nothing to fear. I promise." He dipped his head and brushed his lips over hers. "Say it, Phoenix. Say the words now."

"I...love you, Kai." She whispered back. "With all my heart."

Victory!

Hot coals swirled to life in his belly. He took a step back, and another, holding her soft brown gaze with his. "I promise."

He stretched his arms out, tipped his head back, and welcomed the consuming heat of the flames.

Nixy shook her head in denial as her stomach roiled. Until this moment, the most terrifying thing to happen to her was being cornered by a group of reporters on her way home from school when she was nine. And the most soul-crushing moment had been sitting next to Efrem's hospital bed as he died.

But, this—watching Kai being consumed by bright red and purple flames, feeling the flash of heat over her skin and being helpless to stop it—was far worse.

Get the fire extinguisher, idiot.

She scrambled out of her chair, but it looked like it was too late. The flames had already ebbed, licking over the smooth surface of a huge gray-black egg like eddies of an outgoing tide. The thing was the size of three footballs, and was all that was left of Kai.

A whimper rose in her throat as she lowered herself to her knees next to the egg.

"What the ever-loving hell, Kai?" And what was she going to do now?

I'm alone again.

Just like before, with the shattered remains of her heart stabbing at her soul. A high-pitched laugh of irrational panic escaped her, the sound of hysteria and denial. Because who came back from being incinerated like that? No one.

A convulsion rocked her body as her whole world narrowed down to the silent stone-like egg on the floor. And she gave herself over to dark grief, letting it swallow her up.

Swoosh.

"Ms. Vogel?" The deep voice called her through the blackness, and awareness of her surroundings creeped back.

Her office, the desk drawer handle digging into her back, the floor under her numb butt cheeks, and the warm weight of something in her lap.

It's the egg...Kai.

She stroked her hand over its smooth surface. It was gorgeous, like a piece of polished obsidian. Except not as inert as it'd seemed. Purple and red flames danced under its surface, following her fingertips.

Purple, like his eyes.

"Ms. Vogel?" The voice again.

She leaned her head back against the desk and stared at the black-winged Bezchian kneeling next to her. Fyad. The bodyguard.

She ran her tongue over her parched lips. "Was I supposed to call you?"

Her voice was rough, as though she had been screaming. Had she screamed?

Fyad shook his head. "Raven and I are here to help you now. Do not worry."

"I...I guess I'm just one of those people destined to love and lose." God, that sounded so fatalistic.

"No." His firm grip on her shoulder snapped her back from sinking into the depths of self-pity. "This is just a temporary situation for Elder Kai. We will get him back as soon as we can."

Just as Kai had promised. A tiny kernel of hope sparked in her heart. "He'll come back."

"Yes."

"Because," she smoothed her hand over the egg's surface again, "he's a phoenix, right?"

"Exactly. This is his rebirth."

A familiar young, black-haired woman peered at her from between the top of Fyad's wing and his head.

"Hi, I'm Raven." Raven's smile radiated confidence. "Everything's going to be okay, Ms. Vogel, trust me. His Elderliness has a plan."

The spark of hope blossomed and an edge of determination took root. "What do we have to do?"

"First," Fyad glanced at the egg, "we need a fire pit or wood-burning oven."

"I have a brick barbeque in my backyard. Will that work?"

"As long as we can light a fire in it." Fyad turned partway around. "Raven, would you grab the cinnamon?"

Oh, right. The bag Kai had brought was still on her desk. "What's that for anyway?"

"Phoenixes rejuvenate in a nest of a rebirth spice called cinbin." Fyad rested his hands on each curved end of the egg. "Your cinnamon is identical to it. Ready to go?"

She shooed his hands away. "Yes, but I'm not letting go of him. Raven...?"

"I'm here." The young woman stepped into view again.

"My keys are in my purse in the bottom drawer. You're driving."

It took twenty minutes to get loaded and back to her place. Fyad had to fly because he didn't fit into her compact car. Once they'd reconvened on her enclosed back patio, Fyad removed the barbeque grills and fussed with the cinnamon, spreading it in a thick layer across the bottom.

"Smells like Christmas out here." She murmured the

words as she lowered herself to perch on the end of her chaise lounge.

Raven chuckled as she sat next to her. "Nothing wrong with that."

She trailed her fingers over the egg again. "I swear the flames follow my fingers."

"What flames?"

"The ones just under the surface, see?" She moved her hand so the young woman could see.

Raven leaned close, then shook her head. "Looks like a giant, polished, black glass egg to me."

Fyad stood up and brushed his hands together. "It could be that only the soul mate of a phoenix can see flames." He gestured toward the barbeque. "It is ready, Ms. Vogel. Set the egg down gently in the trough in the center of the cinnamon pile."

But I don't want to let him go.

But Fyad was the Bezchian expert here. The one who'd received a crash course on phoenix rebirth just hours before Kai had come to her office.

"Here we go, Kai." She hoisted herself to her feet, pressed her lips to the egg's warm surface, then settled the egg in the bowl scooped out in the middle of the cinnamon. "Now what?"

"What time did he combust?"

"In the car, she told me it was around seven twenty," Raven said. "And it's just after ten now, so we should light him up Sunday evening."

"Light him up?" That sounded counter intuitive. She moved her gaze from one to the other. "He's already spontaneously combusted once. Please don't tell me he has to do it again. And why Sunday?"

That's six days away, for crying out loud.

"He needs the heat to hatch," Fyad said. "And during rebirth, his kind age backward at a rate of roughly three sun migrations per day, which would take about twenty-four days. However, Elder Kai does not wish to rejuvenate to infancy this time, so we will force early rebirth by lighting the egg."

She should get this, but her brain had taken a self-imposed timeout. "Nope. Still don't understand."

"It means," Raven took her hand between her own and patted it. "His elderliness wants to rejuvenate to be the same age as you. In six days from the time he became an egg, he'll be fifty-five. Your age."

Wonder filled her. "Oh! That's…that's…."

"…the most romantic damn thing ever." Raven nudged Fyad in the ribs with her elbow.

Yes. Yes, it was. As long as she didn't miss ignition time, everything would be okay.

FOURTEEN

---*---

Sunday.

"This has been the slowest six days f my life." Nixy ran her hand over the phoenix egg sitting on her outdoor barbeque. The internal flames still chased her hand like a plasma ball. "But, if everything goes as planned, we'll see each other again this evening."

What she needed was a solid night's sleep—preferably with Kai next to her, in her bed. The chaise lounge was not comfortable by any stretch of the imagination. But it was close to Kai, and for that reason alone, she'd keep sleeping on it no matter how long it took him to *hatch*.

"Fyad and Raven have been so sweet to me since you morphed." Because that was an easier word to wrap her head around than exploded, or combusted. "They bring me food and sit with you so I can nap. They're back at the suite making lunch right now. Fyad did a good job explaining what was happening to you. Including the part that you will be mortal."

That was something she should've asked Kai about *before* professing her undying love. She'd damn near lost it when it'd occurred to her that eventually she'd die, and he'd rebirth. But Fyad swore Kai would come back *mortal*.

"Let's see, what else? Did I tell you that Adam convinced Jordan, my supervisor that I had worked myself to exhaustion? He got her to reschedule our meeting and give me the rest of the week off."

Adam deserved a damn bonus and a pay raise, which she'd discuss with Jordan at their rescheduled meeting in a couple of days.

"I have been working on my resume, though. May as well have that together. Also, Fyad contacted your clan. He told them everything except where you are, and your most esteemed elder flipped his lid. Fyad's been super-protective of you." Thank God the trade negotiations had been put on hiatus until Prime Advisor Rol returned from Bezchi. Everyone was too distracted by that scandal to even notice the phoenix egg chillin' on her barbeque. "Oh, and he told me there's a new baby phoenix in your colony."

"Who in the world are you talking to over there, Nixy?"

She jerked her head up at the unexpected voice. Her gaze landed on the tiny elderly woman standing on the other side of her backyard friendship gate. "Myself, as usual, Mrs. Lentz."

Yeah, crazy lady talking to an egg, here.

Not that her cute little neighbor could see it inside the barbeque, but still.

Mrs. Lentz laughed, her thinning white hair bright under the autumn sun. "The story of my life, dear. Do you need any eggs? My girls have been working overtime and I have more than I can use."

"Sure." Kai might be hungry after he hatched. If he ate eggs. That was another question to ask Fyad when he got back. She should write it down so she didn't forget.

"I'll put them by the gate." Mrs. Lentz waved and made her way back into her garden.

"I think you'll like Mrs. Lentz, Kai. She's a sweet neighbor, always looking out for me, and all. We're both widows, so it's been nice to have her company." A sympathetic ear, and someone who really understood.

She bent and pressed her lips to the warm surface. "No matter what happens, I'll still love you."

In just six more hours, give or take, she'd be able to tell him that in person, again. Seven-twenty couldn't come fast enough. She lowered herself on the edge of the chaise, swung her feet up, and grabbed a home improvement magazine. Had to do something for the next few hours, may as well read.

Within moments, her eyelids grew too heavy to keep open.

She opened her eyes and gazed up at a sky so blue it bordered on sapphire.

"Wow." She breathed the word out.

The closest she'd ever seen a similar color sky was the summer she'd visited the Rocky Mountains in her twenties. Even then, it didn't come close to the jeweled tone of this sky.

A whir reached her ears, and some sort of golden beetle flew over her head. She rolled onto her side to watch it, propping her body up with her elbow. The insect circled a patch of tall orange wild grass before disappearing into it.

Where am I?

She let her gaze roam over the unfamiliar garden. It was like a southwestern desert, except rather than pastels, everything was jewel tones. The amethyst and ruby succulents, carnelian shrubs, and short, emerald-fronded trees—all were rich and vibrant.

Even the stone she lay on was a brilliant white, as if it wouldn't be outdone by its lack of color.

"What is this place?" Another dream, maybe?

"It was my home for almost four hundred sun migrations."

That sounded like Kai. She sat straight up, heart racing as the source of the beloved deep voice came into view, striding toward her along the sandy path. He was different, younger than he had been before he'd blown up in her office. No more than a couple of years older than her. He even moved like a younger man, more fluid, his yellow pants billowing around his legs.

And, hell's bells, those abs of his were more defined than before, too. Try as she might, her mouth didn't seem to want to work right, or form coherent words. Then, Kai was there, sitting next to her on the stone, close, but not touching.

"How are you, my flame?"

"A-as good as I can be after watching you spontaneously combust right in front of me. And you?"

"Eager to be out of my shell." He grinned. "Eager to hold you...*real* you...again."

"Me too." She moved to slide her leg over his and straddle his lap. "Because that kiss you gave me in the office...mm-mmm."

"Aye." He brushed her hair back behind her ear.

She frowned at him. "Your clan says they want you back. They want to send someone to bring you home."

"Pah, just a lot of blustering. My home is on Earth, with you. Once I have rebirthed, our most esteemed elder will be forced to concede."

"Are you sure?"

"I am. Remember the new baby phoenix you told me about—"

"You *heard* that?"

He gave her an *oh, come on* look. "I have heard every word you have spoken since becoming an egg."

"Wow. I had hoped, but I didn't know. So, what about the baby?"

"It is my successor. The colony must have a consistent number of phoenixes, and nature has always provided."

"So," she wiggled on his lap, "two phoenixes did the wild thing and had a baby?"

His laughter was clear, and the garden seemed to brighten for it. "No. Phoenixes can only mate with their soul mate, and our soul mates are never another phoenix. New phoenixes come from the clans. I came from the Landwalker clan."

"Wait a minute. You're telling me that two regular ol' Bezchians from the Landwalker clan gave birth to a phoenix?"

He nodded once.

"And they just handed you over to the elders?"

"Aye. It is a huge honor to be the life givers of a phoenix."

"Huh. Well, I guess so." They were going to talk about that more later. "I wouldn't be very happy if I had to give up my baby."

"I was never theirs. An implicit fact all Bezchians are aware of."

"Still don't get it. I have a feeling I'm in for some culture shock when this is over. So, how do you know the new kid is your successor?"

"When a new addition comes to the colony, it means that one of us is about to leave, or has left already. In most cases, it is because the one leaving has found their soul mate." He nipped at her chin. "And that is why you must wake up now."

"Huh?"

"Wake up, Phoenix Vogel." He took her by the shoulders and gave her a gentle shake. "Something is wrong, and your help is needed."

"But—" She wanted to stay here, with him.

"*Go!*"

"Wake up, Ms. Vogel." Someone was shaking her as she surfaced from the dream.

"Uhhh."

"Hurry." The urgency in the voice cut through the fog of her nap. "We have a problem."

"Fyad?" She forced her eyelids open and her gaze went

immediately to Kai's egg. It looked perfectly fine. "What's the problem?"

She swiped the back of her hand over her cheek drool. Ick. That was so not sexy.

"Prime Advisor Rol is back." Fyad squatted next to the chaise lounge, his black gaze more intense than usual. "He is demanding to see Elder Kai."

Everything rushed back like a tsunami coming ashore, and fear wrapped its barbs around her heart. "His clan wants him to bring him back?"

"That is my suspicion."

"Crap-o-la." She pushed herself upright. "Where's Rol now?"

"I left him and his mate, Ms. Faulkner at the Silverstar suite. Raven is distracting them so we can move Elder Kai before they take him."

Over my dead body would that happen. "Or, we could light him now."

Which made more sense. Kai couldn't fight extradition if he was an egg. She scrambled off the lounger. There was a stick lighter somewhere in the barbeque cabinet.

"But, it is too early," Fyad protested.

"Screw that. It's harder to carry away an unwilling person than an egg." She yanked open the cabinet to the right of the grill and peered inside. "Got it."

Fyad's large, muscular arm snaked around her waist and swung her away from the barbeque.

"*Eep.* Dammit, Fyad!" He was holding her up so high she couldn't touch the ground. Instead, she kicked her feet. "Put me *down*, you big bully."

"Not until you listen."

"We don't have time for this." *Kai* didn't have time for this.

She wiggled like a fish in a net, but it was no use. It was Fyad's way or the highway. If only she was thirty years younger, and a man. A really big man. But, if she was, they wouldn't even be here.

She let herself slump in his grip. "Fine. I'll listen."

Fyad set her on her feet, and turned her to face him, his huge hands clamped around her shoulders. "I believe I got away from the suite without the prime advisor following."

"Are you sure?"

"Yes."

"What time is it?"

He glanced over her head to where the clock was. "Two-thirty."

"Four hours. That's less than two years to go. Fifty-seven is close enough to fifty-five."

"Yes, but that's not what—"

A loud screech filled the air, and every hair on her arms stood on end at the sound of a predator cornering prey. Something large and dark hurled to the ground, landing on her grass with a thud that vibrated the paving stones under her feet. Then Rol straightened up from his crouch and regarded her with solid black eyes, no whites showing.

Well, crap. Her heart plummeted to her stomach. How could she fight off someone so much bigger and stronger?

Rol inclined his head in the direction of the barbeque. "Is that the elder?"

She stepped between him and the egg, and raised her chin.

"Why do you want to know?"

The corners of his stern mouth twitched as though he was suppressing amusement at her blatant stalling tactic. She ground her teeth together so hard it was a miracle her fillings didn't pop out. That arrogant jerk could move her as easily as Fyad had, but that didn't mean she'd give in without a fight.

Fyad moved to her side. "How did you find us?"

"Hunting vision." Rol blinked, and his eyes returned to normal—one gray and one blue. "And superb hearing. You left the suite too soon, Fyad."

"What do you mean?"

"He means..." A familiar older human woman with a cascade of golden curls strode around the corner of the cottage. "...that he should've talked faster so you'd all know that I spent the entire trip back to Earth combing through Bezchian law to make sure I could cover your asses if the Firewings tried to lodge a formal protest to your match." Meryl Faulkner came to a stop next to Rol and gave him a critical once-over. "You sure love your grand entrances, don't cha, big guy?"

Rol gazed down his nose at Meryl, his eyes sparkling with mirth.

That almost sounded like a good thing. Like maybe Rol wasn't here to take Kai back to his clan. "So? What did you find out? Can they take him away?"

Meryl shrugged her shoulders. "They might *think* they can, but by the time they find him, he'll be hatched already. Not a damn thing they can do about it then."

"How did you find out the elder and Ms. Vogel are soul

mated?" Fyad asked, his eyes narrowed in suspicion. "I am certain Elder Kai did not know himself until last Monday."

"That was me." A timid voice pulled her attention to Raven, standing at the same corner Meryl had just come around. "I'm sorry, Fyad, but I used the deep space communicator to contact the prime advisor for help."

"It is Representative Rol, now," Rol corrected.

Raven nodded. "That's right. And he'll be the Bezchian Intergalactic Trade Guild's spokesperson on Earth once the trade agreement is ratified." She wrapped her arms around her middle and focused on Fyad. "Are you mad?"

The corners of Fyad's mouth rose in a slow grin and he spread his arms. "I am proud of my little reporter."

A silly grin blossomed on the young woman's face and she ran straight into his embrace.

"Well, Ms. Vogel?" Rol folded his arms across the wide expanse of his chest. "None of us have had the honor of witnessing the rebirth of a phoenix. Is it really time to light him now?"

"Not exactly." She quickly explained the logistics of years and days, and Kai's wishes on the matter, as Fyad and Raven backed her up. "So, we should actually do it between seven and eight this evening."

Meryl made a fist pump. "*Yes.* This'll be over before anyone is the wiser. Would it be okay if we stayed?"

"I guess." After all, it wasn't every day that a phoenix hatched on her barbeque.

The afternoon passed by in a blur of conversation, and eventually dinner—served on her best paper plates, of course. The whole time her gaze kept going back to the fluttering flames, which seemed to get progressively brighter and more active than the flickers they had been the past few days.

"Earth to Nixy."

She turned her attention to Raven. "Huh?"

"It's seven fifteen."

"Oh." Her heart thumped harder as anticipation gripped her by the chest. *It's time.*

She launched herself toward the hearth, accompanied by the amused chuckles of her friends. It was wonderful how that sound lifted her spirit. Or, was that because Kai would be with her again in a few minutes? She pulled the door of the built-in cabinet open, and there it was, her stick lighter. In fire engine red, of all colors. How appropriate.

She drew it out, wrapped her finger around the trigger, and pulled it back. *Click.* The little yellow flame danced on the black tip of the lighter. She stepped closer, and lowered it to the underside curve of the egg.

Nothing happened. "C'mon, c'mon, c'mon."

Fwump!

Purple and red flames engulfed the entire egg. A collective *ah* came from the rest of the group as she took a step back from the heat.

Wow. It really is beautiful.

The mesmerizing flames grew taller, nearly as tall as the brick chimney; then sparks shot straight up into the air, snapping and crackling.

Rol stood up, his expression grim. "Everyone, step back."

But her feet refused to follow the order, and somehow that didn't concern her. Not with the stunning pyrotechnic display ramping up in her barbeque.

"Come on, Ms. Vogel." Fyad's meaty hand closed around her biceps and he tugged her toward the back wall of her house.

"But, why—"

BOOM!

A scream escaped her as she was thrown face down, pinned to the patio stone by Fyad's weight. Chunks of bricks, mortar, and flaming eggshell rained down around them like Armageddon. Above her, Fyad made an occasional grunt of discomfort. Poor guy was taking the brunt of the fallout to protect her.

Then, it was over. The silence was almost complete, except for the sputtering hiss of dying embers. Fyad's weight disappeared, and suddenly she could breathe again.

She rolled herself into a sitting position. "Holy *moly*."

Her brick barbeque looked like Godzilla had taken a bite out of it, and the shattered chimney debris was strewn across the backyard. Thin whisps of smoke rose from a smattering of black burn holes in the chaise lounge's cushion, and the scent of burnt cinnamon hung in the air. Yet after all that, her house was still standing. In fact, it didn't seem to have been affected at all.

Raven and Meryl peeked out from under the protection of Rol's wings.

"Well, shiiit," Raven breathed.

That was an understatement, but, yeah. Shiiit. She peered

through the clearing haze of smoke, and her attention zeroed in on the figure crouching, head bowed, in the middle of what had once been her barbeque.

"Kai." She'd barely whispered his name, but he jerked his head up and locked onto her gaze. Her heart seemed to do a loop-de-loop in her chest at the intensity of love in his deep violet eyes. "Oh, my."

All the lines and creases on his face had been smoothed away. Now, no more than a hint of crow's feet crinkled the corners of his eyes, and laugh lines bracketed his mouth. But where were his beautiful wings?

"Kai, your wings are gone." The sadness of his loss blanketed her.

Kai rose to stand, and wings of flame unfurled behind him in magnificent glory. If not for the bright red headfeathers, he could be an avenging angel. One who was as unconcerned as a newborn that he was buck naked. She let her gaze track down his body—*whoa*. Naked, and ready for action.

A pulsing need came to life in her core. Apparently, he wasn't the only one looking for action. She shifted her butt from one side to the other, but it did nothing to relieve the growing ache.

"Okee, time to go." Meryl grabbed Rol by the hand and led the bemused Bezchian out of the backyard.

Fyad stood and brushed himself off. "Welcome back, Elder Kai. Come, Raven, I need help attending to my back and wings."

Seconds later, it was just her and Kai.

Naked Kai. Yummy naked Kai with a full-blown hard-on, striding toward her like a man with a purpose.

He stopped in front of her and extended his hands. She automatically grasped them and allowed him to tug her to her feet, bringing her face within centimeters of his.

"Hello, Phoenix." His voice was rough with need, making her given name sound beautiful for once.

It was enough to melt her girly parts. "Hi there, handsome. Nice wings."

The flaming appendages disappeared, and a small gasp popped out of her. "What…?"

"It seems I am able to turn them on and off at will."

"Well, *that's* cool."

"Nixy, dear?" A concerned female voice from the back fence sent a cringe through her.

Kai's mouth twitched with suppressed amusement as she leaned to one side to see around him.

Opal Lentz peered over the back gate. "Is everything okay? I heard an explosion."

"Yeah, sorry. Just a, um, science experiment gone haywire."

Opal's gaze lowered to Kai's butt. "I can't wait to read the lab notes for this one."

Heat burned her cheeks, but her neighbor grinned and turned back toward her own house. Well, that was…awkward.

Kai dipped his head until his lips hovered over hers. "I may owe you a new outdoor barbeque."

"The old one sucked, anyway."

Then his mouth was on hers, nipping, tasting, exploring, as her senses whirled into chaos.

FIFTEEN

---✦---

Nixy sat back in her office chair, not breaking eye contact with her supervisor across the desk. On the one hand, it was a relief to have the truth about the application out there finally. But now, the ax was going to fall.

The expression on Jordan Jones's face was one of incredulity. "Well, Nixy, that was unexpected. I was coming to offer you a promotion, not fire you."

"You *were*?" Did *not* see that one coming.

"Yes." Jordan shook her head with a dry laugh. "I buy that you submitted the application by accident, but you understand that I can't play favorites."

Yes, there was that. "So, what are you going to do?"

"Good question." Jordan tapped her finger against her full lower lip, her wide brown eyes narrowing as though weighing all her options.

Some people might have a problem having a supervisor twenty years younger than themselves, but Jordan had always been fair and impartial. And, she'd been with Silverstar since it was founded, or so the story went. Still, she sure didn't envy Jordan's predicament. It must suck being the boss sometimes.

Jordan shook her head. "I can't give you the promotion at this time, you know."

"I didn't think so."

"The best I can do is suspend you, with pay, as a disciplinary action. But, you will be able to return to your current position here in, mmm, two weeks. What do you have to say about that?"

She blew out a relieved sigh. "Thank you for not firing me?"

"You're welcome." Jordan rose from her chair and gathered her jacket and briefcase. "That should give you time for a quick honeymoon to Bezchi."

"Yes, ma'am." She pushed out of her own chair and extended her hand. "Thank you, again, Jordan."

Jordan gripped her hand firmly. "I can't afford to lose a dedicated employee like you, you know. We'll talk again once you get back. In the meantime, Adam can pinch-hit for you, I'm sure."

"I can't think of anyone better suited to manage the store." Putting a plug in for Adam could cost her a well-groomed assistant, but he was more than ready to be made a full agent.

One corner of Jordan's mouth quirked up. "I'll keep that in mind." Then she headed toward the door.

"Oh, and Nixy." Jordan turned at the door. "Congratulations on your mating. I'm really happy for you."

The door swished open and Jordan was gone, to be replaced by over six feet of sexy Bezchian goodness.

Kai sauntered toward her, looking mouthwatering in his draping purple leggings and off-white pull-over. No more nayars for him. "Well?"

"Oh, don't try and trick me. I know how good your hearing is."

"I cannot seem to help it." His grin was downright sinful as he rounded her desk. "Congratulations on keeping your job."

"Thanks." She stepped into the circle of his arms and inhaled his scent through her nose. "Mmm, cinnamon. My favorite."

"*You* are my favorite." He dipped his head and pressed his lips to the tip of her nose.

Ooh, something was standing at attention between them. She wiggled closer. "Yeah, well, how did your call with your most esteemed leader go?"

"It went better than I had expected. Uri was skeptical at first, but in the end he recognized the signs for what they are."

"So, he believes we're soul mates?"

"Aye. If for no other reason than it explains Zha's appearance."

"Zha? Is that the new baby?"

"Aye. Also…." He clasped his hands around her waist and lifted her to sit on her desk. "He is considering my recommendation that the elders give priority to finding love mates over arranged mates."

"Well, that's a start at least." She tipped her head to one side as he swooped in to nibble at that special place just below her ear. "How do you feel about going back to Bezchi for a couple weeks?"

"Why?" He worked at the buttons of her blouse with his fingers.

"What do you mean *why*?" She moved her hands to cover his, stopping his progress, at least for a moment. "Your clan is there. Don't you *want* to go see them?"

His gaze met hers. "There is no place for me there anymore. My soul mate's clan is now my clan. Your home is my home. This is where I belong—with you, on Earth."

"But, won't you get bored? What are you going to do?"

"First, I am doing *you*. Right now. More than once, if Adam does not interrupt. After that, I am taking you down the hall to show you my new office."

"Excuse me, what?"

"Jordan offered me a job." He shrugged as if it was no big deal. "And I accepted."

"Y-you mean we'll be working together? Matching people?"

"Exactly." He stuck his hand under her desk, and a soft *snick* from somewhere behind her reached her ear. "Now, my flame, the door is locked, and I cannot seem to get enough of you."

"Oh, you naughty bird." She tugged his shirt free from the waistband of his leggings and slid her hands up his chest and over his nipples. "Just don't forget to restrain your wings, this time. I don't want to have to use the fire extinguisher on your shirt."

"Or I can simply remove it."

"You won't hear me complaining."

His shirt came off in record time, and so did her blouse,

along with her bra. His expression every time her breasts were freed never lost its wonder.

"Ah, Nixy," he whispered, pressing a kiss to the top of each mound. "I come from such a harsh climate, and you are so soft."

He closed his mouth over her nipple, and she tilted her head back and moaned. Softly. Because the walls were insulated, but not sound-proof. Although, the way he swirled his tongue around and nipped at her nipples made every instinct beg to be released in the loudest, most attention-getting manner possible.

Egads, her menopausal self didn't stand a chance against his gentle assaults. He moved back up, claiming her mouth in a soul-shattering kiss, and she was helpless to do anything but fall into it. Let him sweep her away as his hands roamed over her over-sensitive skin, touching and tweaking until she writhed with need.

"Now, Kai." She murmured the words against his mouth.

He turned her around and bent her slowly forward over her desk. Then stroked his hands up her thighs, shimmying her skirt up inch by delicious inch.

"You are not wearing under-garments, Ms. Vogel," he chided.

She arched her back and peered over her shoulder at him. "A girl just never knows when she'll see some action."

His deep growl vibrated against her back as he leaned over her, the touch of his skin against hers dragging another moan from deep inside her. Since his rebirth, his temperature had been a bit higher than before. That had been a disconcerting discovery, until he'd explained that it was his body's defense against the colder weather.

Fall had settled into the area, and it would only get colder. Wouldn't he be surprised when she took him to look at houses in Palm Springs this weekend? It could get cool there during the winter too, but it was still warmer than this side of the mountains.

Kai traced his fingers over her belly and slipped them into her slick folds, finding her clit as though he had a radar for it. A tremor radiated from the point of his firm circular strokes, out through her entire body.

"Kai." She breathed out his name like a plea.

"My Phoenix," he murmured as he pressed hot little kisses and licks along her spine.

"Can't wait. Need you now." Right here, right now, bent over her desk with her bare ass in the air. Screw professionalism. The tip of his shaft bumped against her opening and she arched her back. "Do it."

And he did. He grabbed her hips and slammed into her, rocking her with each thrust.

Oh, my God, those fluttering ridge rings. Hurrah for evolution being so kind to the Bezchians.

She stretched out, the cool glass against her breasts a nice counterpoint to the heat building at her core. She curled her fingers around the opposite edge of the desk, and let her eyes roll upward as Kai pistoned into her. Sweet release cascaded, sending her soaring as if she too had wings. She bit back her scream as her walls squeezed him, and it came out somewhere between a groan and a growl. Kai found his moment two thrusts later, pouring himself into her as she clenched around him again.

The weight of him sagged against her back, and his satisfied sigh filled her with a peaceful wonder. By some quirk of fate, she had been given a second chance at love. She turned her head so they rested cheek to cheek, still joined in the most intimate way as their breath mingled.

Oh, yeah. Life was good.

EPILOGUE

Most Esteemed Elder Uri Firewing propped his elbows on the table and rested his chin on his folded hands. Fya had been right about Kai after all. Shame on him for never quite believing her prediction. In truth, he had not wanted to. Yet, what she had told him hundreds of sun migrations ago was finally coming to pass.

Change.

She had tried to prepare him, to open his mind to make the transition easier, but he had been too stubborn. Her warning words still echoed in his thoughts:

"There is nothing more certain in the universe than change. And change is the one thing all beings resist, even if resistance might kill them. Learn to adapt, Uri, because change is coming."

Change was certainly in the roost now, and Kai had made the first flight for their people. It was both heartbreaking and exhilarating to watch the younger phoenix find his wings and soar.

Now, it was up to the Firewing clan to rediscover their

focus, and Uri was at point to lead them into that new future—or not. The choice was his. A knot of nerves settled in his stomach. How qualified he was to do so remained to be seen.

A soft gurgle came from the cradle in the corner. Zha was awake and would need feeding. He rose and moved to the side of the cradle. The tiny phoenix within blinked his deep lavender eyes, and he lifted the fledgling to his shoulder.

"There now, little one. You have come to us at a great time. Your forebearer left us far too soon, but I hope you stay around longer. Things are about to get exciting."

To my dear readers:

I hope you enjoyed reading *Trail by Fire*. This was *supposed* to be the final book featuring Bezchians in the Silverstar Mates series, but then…something weird happened. Yes! Another story dropped into my head.

I've been working madly though the pandemic to get Ava and Sovah's story out, and discovered a few things that surprised even me. But, before you rush off to pick it up, please let me know what you think of Nixy and Kai's story with a quick review.

Thank you, and enjoy the sneak peek of *Fly With Me*!

~Lea Kirk

*Please turn the page
to enjoy an excerpt from*

Fly with Me
Silverstar Mates

Present day Earth.
(Ten years before joining the Galactic Alliance of Planets.)

"For Chrissake, Regina, what kind of aliens abduct a sixty-year-old woman?" The helpless frustration at her predicament boiled up again in Ava Marie Martin's gut as she stalked a perimeter wall of the gleaming white cell. "*In her hair rollers*, no less."

The hair rollers in question bounced against her thighs inside the overstuffed pockets of her silk bathrobe.

She turned to retrace her steps. "I'll tell you who. *Blind aliens*, that's who."

And I made it so easy for them, didn't I?

Walked right into their trap, then poof, one flash of green light later, here she was, like an extra from *Close Encounters*. Damn putty-skinned aliens with their inverted triangular heads and freaky pewter-color eyes. A bunch of stereotypical Area 51 regulars, the lot of them.

Guess I'm a believer now.

Couldn't really be a skeptic since she'd become one of *those* people. The ones at whom she used to shake her head and roll her eyes. God almighty.

The less than satisfying pat-pat-pat of her bedroom slippers against the black porous floor wasn't helping ease her current pique of temper, either. What she'd give for a pair of spikey, angry-shoes and a solid metal floor right now.

"Cha, honey," Regina Gardenia said from his spot on the floor, somehow still looking fantastic in his vinyl, school-bus yellow mini-skirt and thigh-high boots, even after a week in captivity. "You're as stuck as the rest of us."

Her cellmate had that right. "I know, and it still pisses me off."

There hadn't been a single clue that "Motel Stardust" was actually a spaceship in disguise—parked neatly at the edge of a cracked asphalt parking lot. Who asked questions like that when driving a dark Nevada highway, a hundred miles from Vegas in the middle of the night, anyway? Not her, that was for sure.

"Why? Wait, don't answer that." Regina—aka, Reg "Don't Call Me Reginald" Gardener—waved one manicured hand in the air like the drag queen he was in his Vegas revue. "It's because you have no control over the situation. Am I right?"

She came to a stop directly across the ten-foot cell from Reg, the edges of her silk robe fluttering like bird's wings around her matching cornflower-blue P.J.s. Control *was* at the crux of it all, as it had been for most of her life. She'd worn it like a shield, even when she was quaking in her boots. It'd been her constant companion, facing situations from ridicule and abandonment by certain family members for daring to stand up for herself, to building her multi-million-dollar cosmetics company.

"Okay. You might be right."

"You know I am." Reg nodded as if satisfied with this level of recognition. "We've gone over this before. Being pissed isn't going to do you any good. It's been at least a week, darling. Time to let it go."

"Let her be, Regina." The gentle voice came from the young woman in the second, larger cell across a wide walkway. "There's no set timeframe for going through the stages of grief."

Huh. She frowned and drew her eyebrows together. Leave it to Nora the Wicked-smart Librarian to figure out she'd been following the parameters of grieving, almost exactly. The young woman had a sense of awareness that would've made her an outstanding personal assistant.

Not that I need one of those anymore.

No, she'd sold her business, waved good-bye to her staff, and driven off into the proverbial sunset to retire and enjoy her "golden years." Yeah, that plan was working out just swell.

"Well, if I ever turn into a raging Mama Bear like Ava is now, just bitch-slapped me back to reality, okay?"

Nora snorted. "Reality equals boredom in here. Nothing to do, and no books to read."

Poor kid did look thoroughly bored laying on her back, head propped on the thigh of her buff stud-muffin cellmate.

"Mooo."

The human one, not the bovine. Call *that* rumor confirmed. Not only did aliens exist, they also really did abduct cows.

"Sorry, May Belle," Nora said to the large, straw-color beast nosing at her sandy blonde hair. "You're not boring, sweetie."

The young man gazed down at Nora and cleared his throat in a pointed manner.

"Neither are you, Axill." She patted the muscular forearm resting across her belly.

"Takk," Axill replied in his native Norwegian, then grinned.

Was there a more unlikely pair than those two? The hot, blond actor who played some Norse god from the Cosmos Warriors movies, and the librarian who looked an awful lot like Velma from Scooby-Doo, only with sandy blonde hair.

"Thor is definitely not boring," Regina teased.

"I do *not* play Thor," Axill grumbled.

Nora turned her head to peer at Regina through both sets of light bars holding them inside their respective cells. "He plays Týr, a god originally from Germanic mythology and likely the source of the word Tuesday."

You can take the girl out of the library, but you can't take the librarian out of the girl.

"Cha, darling boy. I know." Regina flashed a teasing grin, his teeth as white against his brown skin as his cotton-blonde wig. "But it's all about perspective. And I for one couldn't care less about which god you portray on screen, I'd still pay to watch *you*, Axill Lund."

Nora's giggle floated from across the cell, and the corners of Axill's mouth twitched upward. Okay, so maybe all of them had bonded to some degree. There was some sort of psychology about that, wasn't there?

She stepped toward the glowing yellow bars of light—not too close, because their shock packed a brain-numbing punch—to study the couple in the other cell. "So, Nora was grabbed leaving her library job at two in the morning, and I got suckered into a fake motel. What about you, Axill?"

The muscular hunk shrugged his wide shoulders. "Between movies, I like to spend time at my cabin outside of Eidfjord. It is remote, no neighbors for a long way. One night, I hear a loud noise, so I go check. It was *them*."

"That sounds like a more classic abduction scenario. Still, I'm sorry you're here." Sorry that any of them were.

"Me too." Reg stretched his long legs straight out, then tugged the tops of his boots into place. "Not that I regret meeting any of you, but getting abducted was a sucky way to end an otherwise fabulous evening for me."

She eyed her cellmate. "Ready to tell us what happened to you, yet?"

"Sure, why not? I'm over most of the humiliation at this point. Especially after hearing all of y'all's stories." Reg folded his hands in his lap. "So, I was on my way back from a cast party and thought I'd found a new pop-up convenience store outside of town. One moment I had my head in the freezer hunting for a pint of Banana Hammock flavor ice-cream, the next, I'm in this cell thinking *da faq*? Actually, I may have screamed that."

"You did." Rather loudly, in fact.

It had been Regina's voice that'd pulled her out of her own vacuum of shock brought on by this nightmare.

"Mooo." May Belle ambled away to the farthest wall from her two people, then proceeded to relieve herself.

"Huh," Nora said. "I didn't think it'd work, but she's getting pretty good at that."

"So, Nora Weber," Reg said in a deeper than normal voice. "You were abducted by a U.F.O., thrown into an alien jail, and traveled to untoward parts of the galaxy that no

Earthling has visited. What was your biggest accomplish-
ment while you were in space?" He schooled his face into a
parody of Nora's shy smile. "I potty trained a cow."

A little snicker bubbled out of Ava before she could catch
it, but it was lost in the raucous laughter coming from Nora
and Axill.

"Thanks, Regina." Nora was sitting up now, her legs
crisscrossed, and waved her hand in the direction of May
Belle's contribution to the floor. "All I can say is that these
last couple of weeks would have been a lot worse if not for
the waste-absorbent floor in here."

"Or, if our cell was as small as Regina and Ava's," Axill
added.

That much was true. Having to pop a squat with no
privacy was bad enough, but at least the waste didn't sit
around on the floor. One of the first things she and Reg did
after waking up in here was to agree on a designated corner
to do their business.

A sense of mild morose settled over her. Damn mood
swings. She trudged over and claimed a spot against the wall
next to Reg. She should be in Vegas with the girls right now,
gambling, going to shows, picking up guys...*celebrating* her
stinking retirement. But now, the trip she'd been planning
for over a year with her besties had gone to hell.

The girls must have reported her missing by now. At the
very least, someone should've found her car sitting in the
middle of the desert. What a shame she couldn't hand that
little convertible over to Robyn like she'd planned. All the
work she'd done investigating how to legally sign it over to
her niece only, and keep Robyn's piece-of-shit husband's

FLY WITH ME

name off the title, wasted. But none of that mattered anymore.

Oh, my poor sweet Robyn.

A sound somewhere between a soft chuckle and a scoff escaped her.

"What's up, honey?"

She raised her gaze and met Regina's. "What do you suppose gray-haired old me has in common with any of you youngsters?"

That caught Nora's attention. The little, bespectacled librarian moved to stand by the light bars of her cell. "You mean, what do four humans and a cow have in common?"

"Yes." The cow who was now receiving an ear scratch from Axill. "What kind of cow is May Belle, anyway?"

"Mooo."

"Hmm." Nora cast a critical eye at the creature. "She might be a Charolais, or maybe a Murray Grey."

"Charolais," Axill said as the cow tipped her head into his palm and closed her eyes halfway.

Regina frowned. "And how does a Norwegian actor happen to know anything about cow genetics, or whatever it's called?"

Axill looked up, gave him a small smile, then returned his attention to the cow in question.

Silence fell over their little cellblock, as if everyone had retreated into their own personal thoughts. She pitched a strand of her chin-length hair and twirled it around one finger. Gray, blond, blonde, off-white—

"Hey," Reg murmured. "Still feeling pissed?"

"Not so much, for the moment." She lifted the curl far

165

enough to give it a critical eye. "But I think I just answered my own question. All of us have light color hair. Including the cow."

"Ha! Not under my wig, I don't."

"True, but do the aliens know that?" She raised her shoulders in a nonchalant shrug.

Nora hummed. "That's interesting. We all have some variant of light hair."

"Well," Regina huffed and touched his fingers to his wig. "If that *is* the reason we were taken, then someone's going to be mighty surprised by me."

"Mooo?"

A shudder rumbled through the floor under Ava's bottom and she snapped her gaze to Regina's. "Did you feel that?"

"Yes." Regina's wide eyes reflected the surprised uncertainty, similar to feeling the first jolt of an earthquake.

Another, harder tremble shook the walls.

She scrambled to her knees and met Nora's startled gaze through the bars. "Has that ever happened before?"

"No."

A high-pitched whine, like over-taxed engines filled the cellblock and the room began to tilt.

I have a bad feeling about this.

"Hang on!" Axill's bellow was barely audible over the mechanical screeching, but it was enough to jar her senses back into place.

Hang on to what? She turned her head in quick jerky movements, scanning the smooth white walls for anything to grab on to, but there was nothing. The floor was a pliable, non-slippery matte material, though.

"Reg, lie flat and try to dig in with your fingernails." She lurched forward, landing belly first on the floor, and her cellmate mimicked her movement by her side.

Everything kept tilting up and up and up, sending her half sliding, half falling toward the dreaded shock bars.

"No, no, no, no." She clawed at the floor, tried to get a grip with her fingers, toes, or heels as she rolled.

A cold sweat broke out over her top lip and her heart pounded against her chest, as if ready to bail on her in an effort to save itself. Just like it did every time she was faced with heights. She caught a flash of bright yellow vinyl and dark flailing limbs, an out-of-control Regina following her silk-covered ass toward the stun-you-stupid bars.

Crap. This is gonna hurt.

About the Author

USA Today Bestselling Author Lea Kirk loves to transport her readers to other worlds with her science fiction romance books. She's the author of the award-winning Prophecy series, and the rollicking romantic Silverstar Mates series about seasoned SFR love, that's part of the Intergalactic Dating Agency series. Why? Because sexy has no expiration date!

Ms. Kirk lives in California with her wonderful hubby, their five kids (aka, the nerd herd), and a spoiled, bossy, yet somehow adorable, pup.

LeaKirk.com